TO PROTECT HIS OWN
Brenda Mott

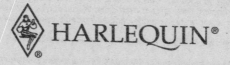

HARLEQUIN®

TORONTO • NEW YORK • LONDON
AMSTERDAM • PARIS • SYDNEY • HAMBURG
STOCKHOLM • ATHENS • TOKYO • MILAN • MADRID
PRAGUE • WARSAW • BUDAPEST • AUCKLAND

ISBN 0-373-71286-3

TO PROTECT HIS OWN

This edition published by arrangement with Harlequin Books S.A.

® and TM are trademarks of the publisher. Trademarks indicated with ® are registered in the United States Patent and Trademark Office, the Canadian Trade Marks Office and in other countries.

www.eHarlequin.com

Printed in U.S.A.

This book is dedicated to the wonderful women
who made my lifelong dream come true:
my editors, past and present–Paula Eykelhof,
Beverley Sotolov, Kathleen Scheibling, Victoria Curran,
Laura Shin–and my agent, Michelle Grajkowski
of Three Seas Literary Agency.
My thanks go deeper than words can say.

PROLOGUE

"Be careful driving home, Caitlin. It's starting to snow." Shauna pulled her head back inside, then partially closed the front door behind the other woman.

"I will. Don't forget—the indoor arena, six sharp." Caitlin pointed an accusing finger at her long-time friend. "No hitting the snooze button. We need to get in one last practice session before I head back to school."

"I'll be there," Shauna promised with a laugh.

Caitlin waved and hurried toward her Pacific-blue Jaguar, parked near the barn a short distance from Shauna Meyers's front yard. As she headed down the dirt-and-gravel road, she flipped the heater on full blast. February in Colorado could be brutal, and it looked like tonight would be no exception. She regretted that she hadn't worn a coat this afternoon when she'd left for Shauna's house. She should've known the fickle mountain sunshine and mid-fifties temperature made no promises. But it didn't matter. The Jaguar X had heated seats, and her long-sleeved sweater was warm enough.

She slid a CD into the stereo, then turned her wipers on as the overture to the *Marriage of Figaro* filled the car. The snowflakes were getting bolder, bigger, and she flicked her headlights to low beam. By the time she reached the two-lane highway, the snow was coming down in earnest. She'd hoped to get home before the roads got bad, but the ranch was a good seven miles from the Meyers's place, and the snow was starting to stick to the pavement. Suddenly her car shimmied. She looked in her mirrors but couldn't see anything. Yet the car handled in a way that told her something was wrong, so Caitlin pulled over to the shoulder.

Nuts! A flat tire. Left rear side. If only she'd taken Dillon up on his offer to teach her basic vehicle maintenance, including how to change a tire. At the time, his big-brother concerns seemed unnecessary. After all, she had her auto club membership. But as she stood in the falling snow, the thought of waiting for the auto club to send someone from town didn't seem like such a good idea after all. At the pace people moved in Deer Creek, it might take a while, and she didn't relish the thought of sitting in her car at the side of the dark mountain highway.

Besides, she realized with a groan, she'd left her cell phone at home. Again. Should she walk back to town and find a pay phone, or stay here in the hope a Good Samaritan came along? The thought was no sooner in her head when a Chevy Blazer eased around a bend in the road from the same way she'd come, and slowed to a crawl. Relieved, Caitlin waved frantically at the driver to stop. But as the Blazer pulled in behind her, the vulnerability of her situation made Caitlin suddenly wary. She relaxed, though, when she saw the lone occupant was a woman who looked not much older than her own twenty-three years.

Before she could make a move toward the vehicle, another SUV rounded the curve in the Blazer's wake, swerving wildly. It crossed over the highway's dotted yellow line, then veered back toward the shoulder of the road. Toward the Chevy Blazer.

Caitlin froze in the headlights.

The SUV struck the Chevy with such force, a deafening screech rent the air, and Caitlin tried to scramble out of the way. Tried to flee from the oncoming vehicles. Everything seemed to move in slow motion as the Blazer skidded sideways and plunged into the ravine below. The dark-colored SUV fishtailed as the driver attempted to correct his mistake in judgment, and struck Caitlin's car.

Her sluggish mind reasoned that even diving into the ravine would be better than being run down. But the Jag clipped her before she could reach safety, flinging her not into the ravine, but in the opposite direction. Onto the highway. She heard squealing brakes and felt intense pain that seemed to wrack her entire body.

Then nothing.

CHAPTER ONE

CAITLIN KRAMER found it ironic that her dreams would be shattered on her birthday. She faced her physical therapist, finally realizing what she hadn't wanted to admit in the six months since the accident. That she would be lucky to even ride a pleasure horse again. She could definitely kiss the Olympics goodbye.

It wasn't fair to take her frustration out on Terri, but Caitlin couldn't hide her bitterness. "Why aren't I getting better? At this rate, I'll never have the balance to ride a show jumper, will I?" She'd hoped the doctors were wrong, and she would be the exception to the rule and heal quickly and completely, returning to her normal self. But the regimen of physical therapy she'd undergone today proved she was the one who'd been wrong.

Caitlin tried to swallow the hot, burning sensation at the back of her throat. Nine days in a coma had left her as helpless as a newborn kitten. She'd spent the first couple of months after the wreck relearning everything. How to walk, sit and eat. How to dress herself. And now this. The painful therapy, which had begun to pay off as she forced her useless muscles to work the way they once had, only seemed to take her so far. But she'd cried enough. She was sick of it. Anger felt like a much better tool.

"You *are* getting better," Terri said. "I told you this isn't going to happen overnight." The therapist rested one hand on the vestibulator—a piece of equipment that reminded Caitlin of an adult-size baby swing. "Do you want me to stop?"

The vestibulator was used to test balance and reflex. A netlike, mesh contraption hung suspended from the top of the metal frame, and Caitlin sat in it, feeling stupid and helpless, like a toddler being pushed by her mother. She couldn't even balance enough to swing independently.

"No. I'm going to do this or die trying."

Terri grinned. "That's the attitude. Perseverance and patience are key to your recovery." She manipulated the machine. "Maybe when you're done here, we'll take you over to my place and you can have a go-round on Jake's bucking barrel."

"Ha-ha," Caitlin said, ashamed of her crabbiness. She seemed to have little or no control over her emotions these days. "Knowing your dear hubby's psychotic obsession with pain, I'm sure he'd love that."

Terri's chuckle was low, amused. "Psychotic obsession, huh?"

"He's a bull rider, isn't he? He's got to be nuts."

"Says the show jumper who sails over seven-foot walls on a twelve-hundred-pound horse."

Caitlin gave her a mock scowl. "I get your point." She held her arms out from her sides. "Let's try this again."

An hour later she sank, exhausted, into her wheelchair. Damn, but it would be good to be rid of the thing. She hated that she still had to use the chair part-time. And feared, deep down, she would never walk completely on her own.

"How'd it go?" Her mother's cheerful voice made Caitlin's spirits sink lower as she watched her step into the room. To have everyone around her constantly acting upbeat and positive got old, even though she knew they meant well. There were days when she wished they'd let her throw herself on the floor and cry like a baby. Days when she wished they'd cry with her.

She looked up into her mother's coffee-brown eyes. "Same torture, different day," she said dryly. "Where's Gran?"

Evelyn leaned over the chair and kissed Caitlin's cheek. "Waiting. She's taking us out to lunch for your birthday. To Bella Luna."

"I don't want to go." She hated going out in public, putting up with curious glances and rude stares. The whispered comments and speculation ate away at what little self-confidence she had left. "Can't we eat at home?"

"No." Evelyn took hold of the wheelchair, and with a goodbye to Terri, began to push Caitlin from the room. "You've hibernated enough. It's time to get out. Get some air."

"I can get air at the ranch." Foxwood Farms had become her haven away from people. Once seen as a local celebrity, now she was only someone to be pitied. She didn't want pity or sympathy. She wanted her life back the way it was before some jerk of a drunk driver had ruined it.

"Come on. It'll be fun."

"Yeah, right. Then the whole town can see how I can barely feed myself, like some helpless infant." Her fine motor skills had not yet returned to the left side of her body. And she was left-handed.

"So eat finger food," Gran said, rising from a chair in the waiting room as Evelyn wheeled Caitlin out. "We'll skip Bella Luna and go to Pearl's Diner instead." Proud and regal like her daughter-in-law, Noreen Kramer was also every bit as stubborn. And every bit as beautiful. Her silver hair curled just above the collar of her blouse. Tall and slender, her peacock-blue eyes sparkled above prominent cheekbones, sculpted not by some clever plastic surgeon, but by Mother Nature. At sixty-five, Gran could've easily passed for fifty.

None of the Kramer women looked their age, including her. Or at least she hadn't before the accident. Now when Caitlin looked in the mirror, the face staring back at her seemed older. And she felt about a hundred.

She rolled her eyes at Gran. "I don't do finger food."

"Well, you do today. Come on." Noreen took over, pushing the wheelchair. "Chicken fingers and French fries sound like a winner to me."

"Ugh." Caitlin wrinkled her nose. "No way am I putting that junk in my body."

Noreen smothered a grin, eyes flashing as she looked at Evelyn. "Listen to her. She actually thinks she's going to win this argument."

ALEX HUNTER slowed his Ford Ranger as he exited the highway. "Are you hungry, Hallie?"

In the passenger seat, his twelve-year-old daughter slumped against the truck's window, staring at nothing in particular. Her long, sandy brown hair tumbled down her back in a waist-length ponytail. At least she'd combed it today. Some days she didn't bother.

Hallie lifted a shoulder. "I guess."

"Pearl's Diner okay? I hear they've got great burgers." He spotted the home-style restaurant up ahead.

She nodded, but her expression said she couldn't care less if they ate hamburgers or rocks.

Alex held back a sigh. Their move from the Denver area a few weeks ago had been tough, but there was no way he was going to stay in the city anymore. Where random violence could change people's lives in the blink of an eye.

"Well, I'm for a double cheeseburger and a chocolate shake." He swung into a parking space behind a sleek black Mercedes and let out a low whistle. "Wow, look at that. Guess not everyone in this town drives a pickup, huh?" He gave her a wink, tipping his new black Stetson, hoping to at least coax a smile from his daughter.

But Hallie remained impassive as she opened the door and slid out. Alex placed his hand on her shoulder as they walked toward the diner's entrance just as two teenage boys came out, laughing and shoving each other. Alex's heart raced as he took in the boys' baggy clothes, earrings and tattoos. He readied himself for the slightest sign of a threat.

One of the boys bumped into him and turned to flash, not a gun, but a smile. "Excuse me." Then they were gone, and Alex let out a breath he hadn't even realized he'd been holding.

Sweat beaded his upper lip and his pulse pounded at his temples. Maybe this hadn't been such a good idea after all. But they were already here, inside the restaurant. His hand still on Hallie's shoulder, Alex made his way toward an empty booth. About to sit, he noticed Hallie staring at something. No, not something...someone. He followed her gaze to a corner table where three women sat—one of them in a wheelchair—and his breath hitched as he stared into the bluest eyes he'd ever seen. Eyes set in a face that could've easily graced the cover of any fashion magazine.

Young, probably barely in her twenties, her hair fell, thick and dark, just past her shoulders. He caught her scowling at him and quickly averted his eyes. But not Hallie. She was still flat-out staring at the woman.

Alex started to reprimand her, but then how could he scold his daughter for doing something he'd been equally guilty of? Embarrassed, he leaned to whisper in Hallie's ear.

"It's not polite to stare." He slid into the booth.

She glanced at him, and for a moment he was afraid she'd retreat even deeper into her shell. The one she wore like a wary turtle, protecting itself from danger. "She looks like Caitlin Kramer," Hallie said, sitting opposite him. "You know...Colorado's Olympic hopeful."

Alex stared at his little girl. This was the longest string of words she'd uttered in a long time. Thanking God and the hoards of horse magazines he'd subscribed to for her—even if she hadn't read them lately—Alex smiled. "Does she?"

Hallie nodded. Then she slumped back against the

seat as the waitress came to bring them ice water and menus. But she kept her eyes on the woman in the corner.

Alex stole another glance toward the table. The young dark-haired woman didn't seem to be hungry, picking at her lunch. The other two looked so much like her, he guessed they must be relatives. Perhaps her older sister and her mother. Or an aunt?

"Hallie, don't stare," Alex quietly repeated, as much to reprimand himself as anything else.

"It *is* Caitlin Kramer. What happened to her?"

Keeping his voice low, Alex pretended grave interest in his water glass. "Let's don't speculate," he said. "It's rude, and besides, that's probably not her, honey." He vaguely remembered Hallie rambling on and on about a grand prix jumping horse and the woman who rode him. But he also recalled she'd been enthralled with the professional barrel racers she read about in her horse magazines, and the high-dollar horses they rode. For months all Hallie had talked about was getting a horse and competing at the Denver National Western Stock Show. Not a practical wish when they lived in the city.

But he planned to give his daughter everything she wanted now that they lived in Deer Creek. If he could have a wish of his own granted, he'd ask for only one thing. To turn the clock back four months and get Hallie out of town before she'd witnessed the drive-by shooting that had taken her cousin Melissa's young life.

The waitress brought their orders, and Alex poured ketchup onto his plate, then dunked a fry in it. Hallie continued to steal glances at the nearby table.

"Maybe you ought to go over there and ask her if she's Caitlin Kramer," Alex said. But even as the suggestion left his lips, he knew it wasn't a good idea. The woman in the wheelchair seemed uncomfortable in her surroundings...any fool could see that.

"Nah." Hallie wrinkled her nose and turned her full attention to her meal, munching fries, wolfing down her huge cheeseburger.

Where did she put it all?

"You want to hit a movie after this? I saw a theatre in town."

She shook her head.

Alex's meal turned sour in his stomach. Hallie was all he had. His wife had walked out on them for another man when his daughter was only three. He'd been the only constant in her life since Julie left. He hated that his little girl's innocence had been tainted by a senseless act of violence. Hated even more that he'd once designed video games that portrayed similar acts. Shoot-'em-up blood and gore. Kill more bad guys, make more points. The more realistic the graphics, the more his games were in demand, which allowed him to provide well for Hallie.

But one bullet had changed his outlook on the business.

He finished his lunch and placed his crumpled napkin on his plate. "Ready to go, Hal?"

"Gotta pee." She headed for the bathroom.

Alex took out his wallet and laid a five-dollar tip near his plate, then tucked a twenty into his hand along with their order ticket. He stood and slipped the wallet back into his jeans, using the opportunity to glance at the corner table. The woman in the wheelchair didn't look at him, but the other two did.

"Ladies." He flashed them a smile and tipped his hat, enjoying his new cowboy gear and the Western tradition it stood for. He'd wanted to fit in with the farmers and ranchers of Deer Creek by dressing the way he had when he was a boy growing up in the mountains.

The silver-haired woman gave him a polite nod, and the other dark-haired lady briefly returned his smile. Confound it. He wanted the young woman to look at him again. Wanted to see those gorgeous sapphire-blue eyes up close.

But she only toyed with the straw in her cup, looking down. Ignoring him.

With a sigh, Alex made his way toward the register near the restrooms to pay for lunch and wait for Hallie.

IN THE LADIES' ROOM, Hallie closed herself into one of two stalls. She waited impatiently for the woman in the next one to hurry up and flush. A few moments later, the sound of water running in the sink reached her ears as the lady washed her hands for what seemed an eternity.

Come on, come on! Hallie stood quietly in the bathroom stall. Listening for the sound of the door. At last the dryer shut off, the door snicked open, then shut with a soft click.

Hallie closed her eyes and focused. She could do this. It was easy, once you learned how. Her friends in Aurora had shown her the way.

She raised her fingers to her mouth and felt her stomach begin to heave in a familiar wave of motion. Then she leaned over the toilet, purging herself of everything she'd just eaten.

But not just the food.

Of everything bad that lay like a thick, black poison inside of her.

CHAPTER TWO

"I DON'T THINK you're ready for this, Caitlin." Evelyn sounded worried, reluctant to let her go. "Why do you have to be so stubborn?"

Caitlin returned her mother's firm stare. "I'm walking on my own now." *Pretty well.* "I'm sick of being smothered. I need my space."

"I don't like the idea of you being alone. What if you fall?"

"I'll get back up." Caitlin folded her arms. "Mom, I'm twenty-three years old. When are you going to stop treating me like a child?" Until the accident, she hadn't realized just how much she'd leaned on her parents, her grandmother and brother. A close family, albeit a rather nontraditional one, they'd never lived far from one another, and Caitlin had spent her entire life at the family's horse ranch—Foxwood Farms.

"You're the one who's acting like a child," Evelyn said, hands on her slender hips.

"Now, girls, let's not argue." Benton Kramer

placed his hands gently on his daughter's shoulders. "Honey, your mother is simply worried about you, and so am I." Six foot two with a sturdy build and silver-streaked black hair, he had the same blue eyes as she did; the same blue eyes as Gran. The laugh lines around them that Caitlin loved so much now crinkled with concern. "Are you sure you're ready for this, peach?"

"Yes, Dad, I'm sure." Caitlin ran her hands up and down his arms affectionately, sickeningly aware of the fact that it took a conscious effort to move her left one. "It's been almost seven months since the accident. And it's not like I'll be far away." The small farmhouse she'd rented was three miles from the Kramers' five-hundred-and-fifty acres. And the house on the neighboring property, which belonged to the Bagley family—longtime residents of Deer Creek—had sat empty, for sale for some time now, so Caitlin would have plenty of peace and quiet. Plenty of seclusion. Exactly what she wanted.

"Okay, then." Benton lifted his hands in surrender. "Dillon and I will move your stuff in this weekend." He ignored Evelyn's continued protests.

Caitlin turned her back on her mother and, with the aid of her cane, headed slowly toward the sweeping staircase and her room.

By Friday afternoon, her things were gathered and she was ready to go.

"Is this it, Cate?" Dillon hefted a box of kitchen goods into his arms. At twenty-six, with coal-black hair and the Kramer blue eyes, he attracted his share of women out on the show circuit. He kept extremely busy, riding, training, showing—their father's right hand in the running of Foxwood Farms. But he'd always made plenty of time for his little sister.

"That should do it." Caitlin felt an exuberance she hadn't known lately as they headed outside. The mid-September heat engulfed her as she headed for her new pickup truck. New to her, anyway.

Her father had offered to buy her a fully loaded, top-of-the-line, dually pickup straight off the show-room floor, but spending that much money on a pickup was foolish. She'd seen the candy-apple-red, '79 Chevy parked at the local lot, owned by a reputable dealer. Something about the way the truck had obviously been lovingly cared for appealed to her.

Caitlin tossed her purse into the passenger seat. She couldn't drive yet. Her ability to perceive distances correctly had been compromised by her head injury. As had her ability to judge the weight of an object. Her brain was left with no way to know how hard to flex her muscles. Without proper balance co-ordination, her brain initially couldn't even communicate the simple act of moving a finger, and it had taken intense concentration and physical therapy to begin to overcome these obstacles.

The Chevy had an automatic transmission. No clutch for her weakened left side. She hoped to be driving within the next month, at least around the ranch.

"You be careful," Evelyn said, giving her daughter a warm peck on the cheek.

Gran hovered over her, fussing with Caitlin's hair, touching her as though she might crumble into dust and blow away on the wind. "Keep that cell phone clipped to your belt, you hear?" She pointed a stern finger. "I know how you're always misplacing it."

"I hear you, Gran." Caitlin smiled and shook her head. "I'll be fine, really. Shauna will be checking in on me, too." Her best friend since fifth grade, Shauna had stuck faithfully by her side ever since the accident, even when she'd tried to push her away. Caitlin kissed her mother and grandmother on the cheek. "I love you both, even if you are a couple of worrywarts."

Evelyn graced her with a good-natured frown. "That's fine. You go on and think that way. We'll see how you feel when you're a mother one day."

But she didn't plan...never had planned...on being a mother. Caitlin herself had been raised by a series of nannies. Evelyn had never been the sort of nurturing mom she now suddenly wanted to be in lieu of Caitlin's accident. Except on the horse show circuit.

Caitlin slid into the pickup, settling her cane against the floorboard. *No.* She'd never be a mother.

She couldn't really relate to Evelyn on a maternal level, and couldn't transfer the concept to herself. Besides, she'd always looked forward to a career as an equestrian with a future in the field of animal science.

What she hadn't planned on was the crash.

Facing forward in the seat, Caitlin looked at the windshield as Dillon drove through the gate and onto the county road. From there, they took a narrow dirt road to her new home. Caitlin noticed that the house on the old Bagley property across the road—a modest, two-story, pale yellow frame—no longer looked deserted…the For Sale sign gone. Curtains hung at the windows, chairs sat on the porch, and a blue Ford Ranger was parked out front.

Huh. She hadn't counted on neighbors, but it shouldn't be a problem. In addition to the narrow road, enough space divided their yard from hers to give her plenty of privacy. Plus, a small area of her backyard was fenced off.

"Here we are," Dillon announced unnecessarily. He shot her the grin that made women swoon. "For what it's worth, Cate, I think you're doing the right thing."

"Thanks." His support didn't take her by surprise, since he'd always been there for her, yet still, it choked her up.

"But that doesn't mean I won't be keeping a close eye on you," he added. Dillon lived on his own horse ranch a few miles from Foxwood Farms, dividing his time between both places.

"Yeah, yeah." Caitlin grinned back at him as he turned off the ignition. But her grin turned to a frown as she opened the truck door and heard a familiar sound. A whinny, and not just any horse. Caitlin froze in her seat, staring at the four-stall barn and adjoining paddock behind the house. Silver Fox trotted back and forth along the fence, then stopped and hung his dapple-gray head over the rail. Ears perked, he stared at her with soft brown eyes, as though asking why he'd been moved from his familiar surroundings with the other horses. "What is Silver Fox doing here?"

Dillon's smile slipped. "What, you're not happy to see him? I thought he might cheer you up."

Caitlin set her jaw. "Take him back to the stables."

"Caitlin…"

"I mean it, Dillon." She got out of the truck and slammed the door, stumbling as she fumbled with her cane. "Dad's going to bring Spike over later once I'm settled in. He's all the company I'll need." The two-year-old Jack Russell terrier had been hers since he was a pup, and his vigorous devotion and enthusiasm helped raise Caitlin's spirits.

"Come on, don't be that way."

"What way?" She whirled to face her brother, the motion making her dizzy. Tears stung her eyes, but she refused to cry. "How could you do this to me?"

Dillon's mouth gaped. "Do what? I was only trying to make you feel at home by bringing your horse over."

"Well, I don't want him here." She clumped up the walkway, tripping on an exposed rock.

Instantly, Dillon was at her side, catching her by the elbow. "Careful." He glowered at her. "Maybe you're not ready for this after all."

"Would you stop treating me like an invalid!" Caitlin jerked out of his grasp. "I don't need everyone hovering over me, I don't need your help walking up to the damned door and I sure as hell don't need Silver Fox reminding me of everything I'll never have again!"

"Caitlin, wait."

But she ignored him, moving toward the house with determination.

THE SOUND of raised voices floated to Alex on the clear mountain air as he stepped outside. He paused in the middle of lifting another sack of groceries out of the truck to listen. Odd. He'd been under the impression no one lived in the white-frame farmhouse. It was why he'd purchased the property across from it. Privacy for him and Hallie. He frowned at the sight of a tall man arguing with a woman who had her back to Alex. She walked with a cane and, as he watched, stumbled and nearly fell. The man took hold of her arm, and the two continued to argue heatedly before she turned and walked away.

Alex hesitated. It wasn't any of his business. But even though he'd moved Hallie away from Aurora knowing the crime rate in Deer Creek would likely be low, he wasn't naive enough to believe that domestic violence didn't happen everywhere. Setting the bag of groceries back in the truck, he crossed the dirt road dividing the properties.

"Is there a problem here?" he asked gruffly as he drew close to the couple.

When the woman stopped and faced him, recognition hit him hard. It was her, the dark-haired, sapphire-eyed beauty he'd seen at Pearl's Diner a few weeks ago. The woman Hallie had insisted was Caitlin Kramer. She was no longer in a wheelchair. He would've smiled if the situation at hand hadn't been so serious.

"No, there's no problem." The man frowned at him. His jet-black hair and row of even teeth said pretty boy. His khaki slacks and polo shirt screamed money, as did his haughty attitude. "Who are you?"

"Alex Hunter." He nodded in the direction of his own house. "I just bought the place across the road."

The young woman raised one eyebrow in a way that sent his libido racing. "I didn't realize I had a new neighbor. The Realtor's sign was still up the last time I was out here."

"I thought your house was empty, too," Alex returned. "We just moved in a couple of weeks ago."

"I'm Dillon Kramer." Pretty Boy held out his hand, and Alex shook it, surprised to find it work-roughened, the man's grip strong and sure. "This is my sister, Caitlin."

So it *was* her. "I've heard of you." Alex nodded and took Caitlin's hand, relieved she was okay.

Her face flushed and her eyes darkened. "I hope you'll excuse me, Mr. Hunter, but I've got things to do."

"Sure. Sorry for the intrusion." He gestured toward his place. "I've got groceries to put away myself." He looked at Dillon. "Nice meeting you. You, too, Ms. Kramer."

"Likewise," Dillon said.

But Caitlin didn't answer. She merely nodded politely, then turned her back on the two men and walked away.

To Alex's surprise, Dillon addressed him softly. "Please excuse my sister's rude behavior. She's not normally like that."

Alex shrugged. "I didn't really think she was rude. I'm the one who barged over here uninvited."

Dillon gave him a crooked grin. "You know, I'm actually glad you did. It'll give me some comfort, knowing someone's nearby to watch out for my sister." He shook his head. "She's very stubborn."

A million questions hammered Alex as he stared at the closed door of Caitlin's house. He knew enough from his daughter's magazines to realize that equestrians of Caitlin Kramer's caliber didn't normally live in a modest old farmhouse. His eyes fell on the tall gray horse that moved restlessly in the nearby paddock. Was it the same animal Hallie had been in such awe of?

"Nice-looking horse," he said. "My daughter's been bugging me for one for some time now."

"How old is your daughter?"

"Twelve."

"Ah." Dillon nodded. "Another young girl bitten by the horse-lover bug."

Alex laughed, warming to the other man in spite of his initial reservations. "A common virus, I hear."

"Oh, yeah. Caitlin was riding before she could walk. Of course, I was, too, so I guess it attacks us guys, as well."

"Yeah." Alex nodded. "I had a horse when I was a kid. But my mom and I moved to Denver when I was in junior high, and that was the end of that." He didn't like to think about how his mother lost their home after his father had died of cancer and the medical bills had eaten up all their savings and then some. Or the way she'd had to work two jobs to make ends meet.

He'd helped all he could when he'd grown old enough to work. He and his mother had had only each other to rely on, just like he and Hallie now did. His mom had passed away when Hallie was five.

"Guess I'd better let you get back to your groceries," Dillon said with a wave. "If you decide to get your daughter a horse, come pay us a visit at Foxwood Farms. We've got some nice ones." He headed toward the house.

I'll bet you do.

Alex stared after him, wondering what Caitlin and her brother had been arguing over. Dillon seemed like a concerned and caring sibling. But then, one never knew what lay behind closed doors.

Alex walked back across the road, anxious to tell Hallie that she now lived across the road from one of her favorite horsewomen.

CAITLIN SAT in the living room, staring out the window. She felt tired, drained both physically and mentally. Her argument with Dillon had depleted her of the last of her energy, and she sat in Gran's old rocker with a teacup of chamomile balanced on one knee, trying to calm her frayed nerves. She sipped from the cup, using her right hand to hold it, her left to awkwardly steady it. Her therapy continued twice a week, and though she was gradually improving, she still wondered if she'd ever be able to do the things she'd once taken for granted.

It broke her heart to see her grand prix jumper standing uselessly in a paddock when he should be in a show ring. Couldn't Dillon understand that the gelding was a reminder of everything she'd lost? Understand or not, at least Dillon had agreed, albeit grudgingly, to get the horse trailer and return for Silver Fox.

Now as Caitlin watched Fox through the window, she saw the gelding's ears perk. He was staring at something and, hearing the sound of a diesel engine, Caitlin craned her neck to see the far end of the paddock. A school bus was pulling away. A little girl, perhaps eleven or twelve, stood on the shoulder of the road, her gaze locked on Silver Fox. She hesitated and glanced toward the house. Caitlin ducked quickly out of view.

When she looked back, the girl was leaning on the paddock rail, talking to Fox. She stroked his nose, then bent and picked a handful of long, golden brown grass and fed it to him. The gelding lipped the treat from the girl's hand as though starved, and Caitlin couldn't help but smile. It brought back her own girlhood fascination with horses.

She set her cup of tea on the round, glass table near the rocker and reached for her cane. Despite her exhaustion, she moved toward the door. Outside, she called to the girl.

"Hi, there. You must be my new neighbor." She hadn't realized Alex Hunter had a daughter. Did he also have a wife?

The girl's head snapped around, sending her long ponytail swinging, and her amber eyes widened as she looked at Caitlin. An odd expression crossed her face, and she pressed her lips together but said nothing.

"It's okay," Caitlin said. "I don't mind if you feed my horse." She walked excruciatingly slowly toward the paddock. "My name is Caitlin. What's yours?"

For a moment she didn't think the girl was going to answer. Long lashes shadowed the child's eyes as she glanced down at her feet. "Hallie." Then she reached up to pet Silver Fox's nose once more. "I know who you are."

"You do?" Caitlin was fully aware her neighbors knew of her aspirations to ride in the Olympics, and she'd been written up in more than one equine publication. Besides, the hit-and-run accident that had nearly killed her had been the talk of the town. She shouldn't be surprised Hallie knew her.

"I recognized you from *Horse Youth* and *Equus.* I used to read them a lot."

Recognition dawned with Caitlin, as well. She'd thought Alex Hunter seemed familiar. She remembered him now, as she looked at Hallie. They'd been in Pearl's Diner on her birthday. Hallie had stared at her until she'd made Caitlin uncomfortable, overly conscious of her wheelchair and her limitations. They might be temporary, but she hated those disabilities, and had no idea how people who were permanently handicapped coped.

"I know you, too. Or at least, I've seen you before." Caitlin forced a smile. "At the diner a couple of weeks ago." Surely the girl hadn't meant to be rude that day. After all, kids would be kids. But she also remembered the way Alex had stared at her. Not like she was a freak, but like he found her attractive. He was a good-looking man himself. But these days she didn't feel much like flirting, and she wasn't sure who had made her feel most uncomfortable, Alex or his daughter.

Elbows hooked through the paddock rails, Hallie looked at the gray gelding. "This is Silver Fox, isn't it." Her words came out not as a question but as a sure statement that she'd just met a celebrity of the four-legged variety.

"Yes, it is. The one and only." She kept her tone light, though her heart felt heavy. She should sell the gelding. He was in his prime and worth six figures. No sense letting such a champion go to waste. The thought made her head throb.

"What happened to you?" Hallie asked abruptly. She looked down at the cane. "You were in a wheel-chair that day at the restaurant."

"Yes, I was," Caitlin said. Deciding forthright was best, she met the kid's honest, open gaze. "I was hit by a car. I suffered broken ribs, a bruised hip, a con-cussion and a compression fracture in my spine."

Hallie frowned. "What's a compression fracture?"

"It's a break…it means I have to wear this back

brace for another four weeks," Caitlin said, lifting the tail of her shirt to expose the stretchy material that bound her like an old-fashioned girdle.

"Will it get better?"

"Probably." But there would be residual pain, the doctor had warned.

"So then you'll be riding in the Olympics?"

Caitlin pursed her lips. "Afraid not, kiddo." She tapped her temple with one forefinger. "The concussion messed up my sense of balance. I can't ride at all." Hell, she could barely walk.

"So who's going to ride Silver Fox?" Hallie asked.

Who indeed? *Not me...* Caitlin pushed the hated words from her mind. "I don't know yet. My brother is going to pick him up today and take him back to my parents' Thoroughbred ranch."

"He is?" The child's face fell.

Before Caitlin could answer, a rich, deep voice cut in. "Hallie, are you bothering Ms. Kramer?"

Caitlin turned to look over her shoulder at Alex, noting for the first time how dark his eyes were. How his hair was almost the same shade as her own, what she could see of it from beneath his black cowboy hat. In faded jeans, a Western shirt and cowboy boots, he looked every inch the rodeo cowboy, right down to the big oval buckle at his waist. It bore the outline of a quarter horse and, to her surprise, was engraved like a trophy buckle. She wondered if he'd actually won it. She hadn't noticed any horses at his place.

"She's fine," Caitlin said. With effort, she looked away. The cane and her left arm, curled awkwardly at her side, made her self-conscious. She hadn't even bothered with makeup since the accident, and her hair was in a careless ponytail much like Hallie's. She looked more like a high school kid than a senior in college.

Former senior. For the millionth time, Caitlin cursed the drunk driver who'd shattered her life and murdered the unborn baby of the Good Samaritan in the Chevy Blazer, a woman who'd been five months pregnant.

"She knows better than to trespass," Alex said, breaking her from her thoughts. But his tone wasn't harsh, his voice conveying the love and pride he felt for his daughter. He grinned. "But then, so do I. Sorry about the misunderstanding earlier."

Caitlin shrugged. "No problem." She really didn't want to get into her personal issues with a stranger. She wished Dillon would hurry up and get here, and take Silver Fox away. Then she could hide in the house and lick her wounds the way she liked best. Alone.

The three of them stood in awkward silence for a moment before Alex spoke. "Come on, Hallie. Let's go home and fix some lunch."

But the child ignored him.

He frowned. "Hallie?" He took a step toward the paddock.

To Caitlin's shock, when the kid faced him, a single tear slid down her cheek. "I don't want lunch," she said. "I only wanted to feed the horse." Her eyes accused Caitlin. "But he's leaving, too. Everyone always leaves." She jumped down off the fence and raced across the road and through the barbed wire fence around her dad's property, disappearing over a rise in the ground.

"Hallie!" Alex called after her. He muttered, "I'm sorry," then took off in pursuit.

Caitlin stared after them. What in the world was that all about? From the paddock, Silver Fox nickered softly.

"You're always hungry, aren't you?" Hobbling closer, she leaned the cane against the fence and cupped the gray's head lovingly between her hands. He lowered his neck over the fence, rubbing against her. "Quit it," she scolded him affectionately, scratching his jaw and the side of his face with her fingertips.

She buried her face in his forelock, inhaling the sweet scent of his coat, which was already turning fuzzy with the coming fall. Prior to the accident, she'd always kept him blanketed and in a warm stall to prevent his winter hair from coming in thick so he'd look good in the show ring. But once she knew their riding days were over, she'd instructed the stable hands to turn the gelding out on nice days to gradually acclimate him to the outdoors. No sense in keeping him cooped up now when he needed the exercise of roaming free in the pasture.

No sense in keeping him here, either.

He's leaving, too. Everyone always leaves. What had the child meant? But it was none of her concern. Lord knew, she had enough problems of her own without worrying about some guy and his kid.

Caitlin felt a pull of sadness as she stood there. It wasn't Silver Fox's fault she couldn't ride him anymore, and she shouldn't take her spite out on the horse. She'd missed him during the weeks she'd spent in the hospital and in her bed at home. And unless she made a definite decision to sell him, there was no sense in shuffling the horse from one handler to another, one place to the next. She might not be capable of riding, but surely she could manage to feed and care for one single horse.

Perhaps with the help of a little girl who obviously had issues, and who maybe needed a friend. She ignored her wicked inner voice that reminded her the girl also had a handsome-as-sin father and most likely a mother.

It didn't matter. No man would ever find her attractive again. Who in his right mind would want to take her to bed and look at her ugly, scarred and twisted body? It had been a while since she'd had a serious relationship. She'd chosen to focus on her horses, her riding and her studies. Thought there would be plenty of time for love later on.

Now all that had changed. She no longer had the career she'd wanted ahead of her, and she also no longer wanted a man in her life. To say she had nothing wasn't fair, because her family loved her, and for that she was grateful.

She stared into the distance where Hallie and Alex had disappeared. Caitlin had thought to hide out in seclusion at the ranch. But something about Hallie had touched her.

Caitlin looked at the horse and sighed. "Maybe you ought to stay here, boy," she said softly. "At least for a little while." At least until she figured out exactly what she meant to do with her life.

Unclipping the cell phone from her belt, she dialed Dillon's number. "Hey, big brother. You can have Dad follow you over here to bring my truck back whenever you get the chance, but forget the horse trailer. I'm going to leave Fox here with me. Yeah, that's right." Dillon's rapid-fire response buzzed in her ear, and she rolled her eyes to the afternoon sky…so clear, blue and vacant above her.

Vacant…

Exactly like she felt inside.

"Yes, I promise I won't try to drive right now. But

I still want my truck." She disconnected, then cane in hand, made her way slowly and painfully back to the house.

CHAPTER THREE

ALEX FOUND his daughter facedown in a patch of grass, sobbing. It was enough to break his heart. He crouched beside her and gently touched her shoulder. "Hallie, honey. Sit up. Come on, baby, let me hold you." He held out his arms, and she flung herself into his embrace. Alex stroked her hair, soothing her until her sobs faded to hiccups and finally to an occasional sniff.

He pulled a clean handkerchief from his jeans and offered it to her. She took it, not saying a word, staring at the expanse of open land that stretched up beyond their property in a carpet of knee-high grass and dense clusters of scrub oak.

"You want to talk about it?" Alex asked. He'd learned long ago from Hallie's therapist to let his daughter work her feelings out, and not to push. But damn it, it was hard to sit by feeling helpless while his little girl hurt so much. He'd only wanted to make her happy by bringing her here to the western slope. And now he wondered if he'd botched that, too. The therapist had warned him that sudden major change wasn't a good idea. But as the months passed, he'd been unable to stand it any longer, not willing to stay in a neighborhood that no longer felt safe.

Hallie shrugged. "I dunno."

He gave her a small smile. "You know, you've been talking to me quite a bit lately, more than you did when we were living in Aurora."

Hallie remained silent.

"I enjoy talking to you," Alex pressed gently. "Like the old days." He'd been her trusted confidant, acting as both father and mother for as much of Hallie's life as she could remember. "What happened back there at Caitlin's? Did she do something to upset you?"

"No." Again, she shrugged her shoulders. "I just thought it was cool to be living next door to her and Silver Fox. I hate it that she's sending him away."

But what Hallie had said—about everyone always leaving—obviously went far deeper than the horse being sent back to Foxwood. Alex stroked his daughter's cheek. "Honey, you know *I'm* not going anywhere, don't you?"

Hallie picked up a twig and traced circles in a patch of dirt near her feet. "Melissa left. And Grandma Hunter. And Aunt D'Ann and Uncle Vince moved to Wyoming."

His gut twisted. Vince was married to his ex-wife's sister, D'Ann. Melissa's parents. Alex slipped his arm around Hallie's shoulders and gave her a protective squeeze. "Not by choice, baby." *Not like your mother.*

D'Ann and Vince hadn't had a choice, either. Melissa's death had destroyed them and they'd been unable to live in the town where their daughter had been murdered. Where so many memories haunted them. They'd returned to Laramie—Vince's hometown.

"No. But that's just it. Sometimes people don't have choices. You don't know what will happen. You can wake up one day and everything's fine—" Her voice cracked and she struggled for control. "And the next minute it's not fine. You're dead or someone you love is gone."

That his daughter should have such a fearful perspective bothered him more than Alex could say. He hated that she lived in a world where violence was common. Hated that he might have in some way contributed to that violence through his video games, desensitizing young people to bloodshed.

And now his twelve-year-old daughter, who should be worrying about boys, clothes and socializing with her friends, was instead worried about death and abandonment.

Alex laid his cheek against Hallie's head. "You know, sugar, there are no guarantees in life. And there's really nothing we can do about that. But there are promises, which we *can* choose to keep." He pulled back and looked at her, hoping she could see in his eyes just how much he loved her. "And I promise, Hallie, I will never, ever abandon you. Not if I can help it. Besides, I'm planning to live to a ripe old age." His lips curved in a teasing smile. "That way I can run off all the boys who come knocking on our door, at least until you're thirty. And I'll do the same for my granddaughters one day."

"Da-ad." Hallie rolled her eyes, and the gesture made his heart soar. To see her do something so normal felt wonderful.

"Well, okay." Alex shrugged. "Maybe just until you're twenty-nine." He stood and took her hand. "Now, come on. You can't sit here crying, or you'll wash away the gully. You might even cause a flood." He kept his voice light, hoping to make her smile.

But there were days when he wished the rain could pour down in a flood to rival Noah's day, and wash away all the things that threatened his daughter and her happiness. He knew he couldn't put her in a plastic bubble or lock her away in a bulletproof room. But he'd be damned if he'd let anyone hurt her. And if Caitlin Kramer was going to make her cry— albeit unintentionally—then he'd have to do his best to see to it that Hallie stayed away from her.

No matter how pretty he thought Caitlin was.

CAITLIN WOKE UP Saturday morning to a cold nose in the middle of her back. She jerked reflexively, arching her back, and a sharp pain shot through her spine. "Damn it, Spike!" Crankily, she opened her eyes and looked at the tan-and-white Jack Russell terrier her dad and brother had brought over when they'd returned her truck last night. The dog wriggled with joy, hopping across the bedcovers like a rabbit on speed. In spite of herself, Caitlin grinned and ruffled Spike's ears. "You've got to learn better bedside manners than that," she said, pushing away the sheet and blanket. Stiffly, she placed her feet on the floor. She looked at the clock—8:00 a.m. No wonder Spike was impatient.

Caitlin went to the back door and opened it for the little dog. She hoped he wouldn't find a way to climb the V-mesh fence. Jack Russells were notorious escape artists. But it wasn't as if she could've stepped outside in her camisole and panties to keep an eye on the dog. Not with Alex Hunter living across the way.

A short time later, Caitlin threw on some clothes and went out to feed Silver Fox, Spike trotting along ahead of her. The gray gelding whickered softly as she neared his paddock. She reached up to stroke his muzzle, planting a kiss on his velvety nose. "What's the matter, boy? Did I wake up too late to suit you?" Fox's normal breakfast time was 6:00 a.m. "Guess I'll have to work on that, huh?"

In the barn, Caitlin leaned her cane against the two tons of hay Dillon had neatly stacked against one wall, near the fifty-five-gallon drums of sweet feed and alfalfa pellets. Even though the bales were somewhat stair-stepped, the ones on top of the pile were well out of her reach. Her brother tended to forget that the rest of the world was not six foot four. Grumbling, Caitlin stepped onto the bottom row of hay and began to climb, slowly, unsteadily, yet pleased she was able to do it. By the time she was within reach of the top row, she was shaking, her hairline beaded with sweat.

But she got a rush from doing the familiar task, one she dearly loved. The sweetness of the alfalfa-grass mix mingled with the clean scent of the wood shavings in Fox's stall—comforting smells she'd known her entire life. Fox had come through the open entrance from the paddock to his stall, and he now nickered at her over the half door. "I'm moving as fast as I can," she called down to him.

Spike had scaled the haystack as though it was nothing more than an anthill. He stood above her, docked tail wagging, his bright, curious eyes seeming to ask what she was waiting for. Caitlin laughed at the little dog, who appeared to be part cat half the time, and reached to grasp the twin loops of nylon twine on a hay bale.

As soon as she tugged it free, she realized her error. This bale likely weighed between sixty to eighty pounds, but Caitlin had completely misjudged it. The heavy load jerked her off balance, and she fell backward, tumbling down the stair-stacked hay. Involuntarily, she let out a shriek.

Spike bounded down and circled her where she landed on the dirt floor, barking for all he was worth. His antics made her all the more dizzy, and Caitlin groaned, clutching one hand to the small of her back. Thank God for the back brace. Still, pain shot through her extremities and her lower spine as she sat up unsteadily. She remained on the floor, trembling, myriad emotions running through her. Anger at her own stupidity. Frustration at not being able to do something so simple. And humiliation at having fallen like a helpless newborn filly trying to gain her legs. She raked a hand through her hair and growled a curse.

"Are you all right?"

Startled, Caitlin looked up into the wide eyes of Hallie Hunter. The girl stood in the doorway of the barn as though unsure of whether to move inside or take off running for help. Her face looked pale.

Caitlin shifted position, then moaned at a fresh stab of pain. "Yeah, I'm okay. Could you please hand me my cane?"

Hallie hurried to get it. She also reached out to give Caitlin a hand in rising to her feet.

"Boy, do I feel stupid." Caitlin gave the kid a crooked grin. "Did you see me fall?"

Hallie's face flushed, and she shook her head, her ponytail swishing. "No. I, uh, heard your dog barking and thought maybe something was wrong." She bent to pet Spike, who leaped all over her with his usual vigor, as if he hadn't seen a human in weeks. The girl giggled as the terrier licked her face. "He's cute."

"He's a handful sometimes," Caitlin said. "But I'm glad he set off the alarm." She hid her embarrassment, knowing the child couldn't possibly have made it across the road so quickly after Spike had begun to bark. She'd probably been lurking in the vicinity to visit Silver Fox again. In all likelihood, Hallie had seen her lose her balance and fall so unceremoniously from the haystack.

"I thought you were going to send Silver Fox to your parents' ranch?"

"Yeah, well, I changed my mind," Caitlin said. "You want to help me feed him?"

Immediately, the girl's face brightened. "Sure."

But before Caitlin could move to cut the twine on the bale that had tumbled to the floor with her, Alex's deep voice carried from across the way. "Hallie! Hallie, where are you?"

"Over here, Dad!" Hallie shouted. "In the barn."

Caitlin's stomach churned. What had she been thinking? That she could befriend the girl and avoid the kid's dad? Self-consciously, she realized what a sight she must look. She'd tossed on a T-shirt with no bra and a faded pair of jeans. And she knew she had hay sticking in her hair, since she was still in the process of picking flecks of leaf and stem from it.

Lovely.

But what did it matter?

You aren't yourself and you never will be. The guy was here for his daughter, not for her. Caitlin faced him as Alex came through the barn door.

"Hi," he said, and then frowned at his daughter. "Hallie, you know better than to take off and not tell me where you're going. I thought we talked about this yesterday."

"Da-ad." Hallie squirmed with obvious embarrassment. Looking up at her father, she quirked her mouth. "I was helping Caitlin."

Caitlin made an effort not to mimic Hallie's squirm as Alex's gaze raked her from head to toe. She picked more hay from her hair. "She's helping me feed."

"Really?" Amusement lit his chocolate-brown eyes and his lips curved, making her heart beat faster. "Looks more like you're wearing that hay than feeding it to your horse."

She rolled her tongue against her cheek. "Yeah, well, I had a little problem pulling that bale off the stack. It more or less pulled me down instead."

Concern instantly replaced his bemused expression. "Are you all right?"

"Yeah. It was nothing."

He glanced at her cane, and Caitlin wanted to melt into the floor.

"You know, if you need help, all you have to do is ask. I can even give you our phone number in case—"

"That won't be necessary." Caitlin cut him off, then realized she sounded rude. "But thanks."

"Oh, I forgot—you're sending the horse away."

"Actually, I'm not." She flashed him a forced smile. "But Hallie and I have things under control here. Right, kiddo?"

"Right." Hallie grinned at her, eyes full of hero worship.

Caitlin was sure that wouldn't last, as soon as the kid realized she was no longer the woman portrayed in the magazines. Ignoring her inner voice, she showed Hallie how to separate the hay into flakes and feed an armful of the large square sections to Fox. She stood patiently while Hallie cooed to the gelding and patted his neck. But her body throbbed, and all she really wanted was to go back inside the house and lie down. She didn't even bother to protest when Alex moved three bales down from the top of the stack to the floor where she'd have easy access to them the next time she fed her horse.

Leaving Silver Fox to his breakfast, Caitlin walked outside with Alex and Hallie, trying to find a graceful way to escape their company. But before she could say a word, Spike suddenly bolted in pursuit of a rabbit that scampered across the open land beyond the barn.

"Spike! Come back here." Caitlin knew it was futile.

"I'll get him," Hallie said, sprinting off after the dog.

"Hallie, don't go far," Alex called after her, his face pinched with worry.

Why on earth did he treat his daughter as though she were five years old? "What grade is Hallie in?" Caitlin asked.

"Seventh." He turned, frowning at her. "What, you're insinuating that I treat her like a baby?"

"I didn't say that."

"You didn't have to." He folded his arms. "You are way out of line, Caitlin. You have no idea where I'm coming from."

She shrugged. "You're right. None of my business." She set a pace she could manage, following Hallie and Spike.

"Wait a minute." Alex stopped her with his hand on her arm.

To her annoyance, every nerve along her skin responded. She scowled at him. "What?"

"I didn't mean to snap at you." He sighed. "I'm sure Hallie will be fine. Let her catch your dog. Lord knows she's got five times the energy I do."

"Kids always have endless energy." Abruptly, Caitlin felt light-headed and shaky.

"Are you all right?" Alex reached out to steady her.

"I'm fine." Doing her best to maintain a casual air, Caitlin walked back toward the barn and sank onto a glider Dillon had installed near the walkway leading from the building.

"You don't look fine," Alex said, sitting beside her.

Sweat beaded her upper lip, and she knew it was a safe bet she'd either gone pale or flushed. "All right, maybe not fine, but I'm okay." She laughed without humor. "Apparently even Spike is more than I can handle. Maybe I should send him and Silver Fox both back to the ranch." She hoped her comment appeared offhanded.

Alex's eyes were serious. "I read about your accident," he said. "Hallie's horse magazines finally caught up with us through our forwarded mail, and I was thumbing through them last night. There was a story about you in *Equus*."

She didn't want to talk about the crash. Hadn't even wanted the magazine to do the article. But Gran had insisted that it was far better to get the facts straight than to leave everything open to public speculation and gossip. She'd wanted it made clear that while the driver of the SUV who struck Caitlin was suspected of—and later confessed to—being intoxicated, there had been no alcohol involved on Caitlin's part.

"Then you know exactly what happened," Caitlin said.

He was silent for a moment. "We had a terrible tragedy in our family about three months after you were run down by that drunk," he said.

Surprised, she looked directly at him. "Oh?"

"Yeah. And since I can't seem to keep Hallie away from your horse, I think it's best you know about it." He took a breath. "My daughter witnessed a drive-by shooting. But for the grace of God, it could've been her who was killed."

Shock gripped Caitlin. "What happened?"

"She and her cousin were walking to a convenience store a few blocks from our house, when kids with a score to settle drove through the parking lot. They fired at some high school boys who were coming out of the store as Hallie and Melissa were going in. They missed the boys but hit Melissa."

"Oh, my God." Caitlin stared at him, not knowing what else to say.

"Melissa was thirteen," Alex said. "She and Hallie were like sisters." He fought to control his voice. "She died right there, while Hallie watched. Bled to death in the parking lot before help could arrive."

Suddenly, Caitlin's own problems seemed petty. "I'm so sorry, Alex." She touched his knee. "I can only imagine what Hallie has been through."

He nodded, glancing down at her hand, and she

quickly removed it. "I don't normally tell my business to everyone. But like I said, if Hallie's going to hang out at your place, I want you to know what she's been through. That's why I'm a little overprotective."

"I completely understand." She felt like an ass for having criticized him moments ago.

Alex nodded, then rose to his feet as Hallie reappeared clutching Spike in her arms. Her smile obviously did Alex's heart good, by the look in his eyes.

"Boy, your dog sure can run. I only caught him because he'd stopped to try to dig that rabbit out of its burrow."

Caitlin rolled her eyes, hoping it would help hide her emotions. That Hallie wouldn't be able to see her empathy. "That's a Jack Russell for you. They'll go to ground after a rabbit or just about anything else they see."

"That's what kind of dog he is?" Hallie asked. "I thought he was a mutt."

Caitlin laughed. "He is. But he's a purebred mutt. They're a pretty popular breed out on the show circuit. Those and Welsh Corgis."

"What's a Welsh Corgi?" Hallie asked.

Caitlin laughed again, enjoying the girl's curiosity. She proceeded to describe the breed.

"Hey, cupcake," Alex said, tweaking his daughter's ponytail. "If you're going to pester Caitlin with a million questions, then the least we can do is offer to feed her." He looked her way. "Your horse has had his breakfast. Have you had yours?"

"No," she admitted reluctantly. The last thing she wanted was to go out to breakfast. Especially with Alex, with his dark eyes and cowboy drawl.

"Neither have we. Why don't you come over and eat with us? I was about to whip up a batch of scratch pancakes anyway. You can even bring Spike." He gave the dog's head a pat.

Caitlin raised her eyebrows. "You make your pancakes from scratch?"

His deep chuckle sent shivers down her back and arms. "What, you don't think a man is capable?"

"No. I mean, yes, I'm sure you're capable. It's just that..." Just that she'd mostly eaten out in restaurants or had her meals prepared by the family's chef. How pretentious would that sound? She shrugged and laughed. "I'm not much of a cook myself, so actually that would be nice." How could she say no? Especially with the way Hallie was looking at her, as though she walked on water.

Her heart went out to the girl. She'd suffered such a horrible trauma. Come close to being killed herself. It was something, regretfully, they had in common.

"Good," Alex said. "Then it's settled. Let's go." He slipped his arm around Hallie's shoulder and began to walk back toward their house.

At least now Caitlin knew the answer to the question at the back of her mind. Alex wasn't married.

As he waited for her to catch up, Caitlin had a nice view of his snug-fitting Wranglers.

Maybe that fact wasn't such a good thing after all.

CHAPTER FOUR

PANCAKES. Alex made them every Saturday, yet he couldn't remember having enjoyed them so much in a long while. He wondered if his pleasure had anything to do with watching Caitlin's face as she closed her eyes and savored a bite of maple syrup-covered, made-from-scratch hotcake.

"Mmm, these are delicious." She opened her eyes and looked at him, smiling. "I don't normally eat such a heavy breakfast, but this is wonderful." She helped herself to a fourth slice of bacon. "Thanks for inviting me."

"You're welcome."

"Dad cooks pancakes all the time," Hallie said, heaping another serving onto her plate. "I love them."

"You'd better slow down," Alex said with a chuckle. "Or we'll have to roll you out the door."

Hallie gave him a mock grimace, swallowing a mouthful. "How many horses do you own, Caitlin?"

"Foxwood Farms has about thirty or forty head at any given time, depending on how many foals we've got. But personally, I've got three. Silver Fox is my grand prix show jumper, then I've got Black Knight—my hunter—and my retired gymkhana gelding, Red Fire. He was my first, and he's a quarter horse/Thoroughbred cross."

Hallie's brows lifted. "You used to do gymkhana?"

"Uh-huh. Barrel racing, pole bending, scurry jump. It was the scurry jump event that gave me the bug to want to become a show jumper. That and watching those classy jumpers at the Denver National Western Stock Show."

Hallie's eyes widened even more. "Dad used to take me to the stock show every year. I love watching the jumpers. And the barrel racers." Her animation made Alex's heart soar. "I want to barrel race soooo bad. Dad says he'll buy me a horse, now that we live in the country. But first we have to fix up the barn."

"Really?" Caitlin paused. "If you're serious, Alex, why don't you bring Hallie out to Foxwood Farms to look at what we have for sale."

"Actually, your brother already suggested that. But I'm not so sure a Foxwood Thoroughbred's in my budget." He smiled, his face warm.

Caitlin's chuckle filled him with a pleasant heat.

"You might be surprised. Not everything on the place is six figures, or even five."

"Thank goodness," Alex said. "I'd hate to have to take out a second mortgage to afford a horse for my kid."

"Dad makes good money," Hallie spoke up proudly.

"Hallie!"

"Well, you do." She shrugged unapologetically.

"What do you do for a living?" Caitlin asked, her curiosity more obvious than her tone of voice let on.

For some reason that pleased him. "I design video games."

"Not violent ones," Hallie said.

Her words hurt. "I used to," he said quietly. "But not anymore." He exchanged a pointed look with Caitlin.

"Yeah, now he just designs boring games rated E for everyone," Hallie said. "But he still makes good money."

Not as much as he'd made in Denver, now that he worked out of his house. But the money didn't matter. His daughter's happiness and safety were all he cared about.

"Good enough to buy a horse?" Caitlin teased.

"Yeah, I think so." He grinned, cutting into another pancake.

"So when can we go look at them?" Hallie practically jumped up and down in her chair.

Suddenly, Caitlin's smile faded, and Alex felt her playful banter wilt like a deflated balloon. "I'll call Dillon and make arrangements for you to see the horses."

Hallie frowned. "Why can't you take us?"

"Hallie," Alex reprimanded, "don't be rude."

"It's okay," Caitlin said, looking at Hallie. "I'm not sure I'm up to showing you around. Your dad can bring you out to the ranch this afternoon though, and we'll see. How does that sound?"

"Cool!" Hallie's face immediately brightened.

Caitlin glanced at her watch. "Speaking of which, I'd better head home. Mom is going to pick me up in a half hour." She grimaced. "I can't drive yet."

"I see." Alex could only imagine how her limitations must frustrate her. "What time would you like me to bring Hallie out?"

"How does one o'clock sound?" Caitlin reached for the pen in the center of the table near the salt and pepper shakers. "If you've got a piece of paper handy, I'll give you directions. It's easy to find—about three miles from here."

"If it's that big ol' place with the wrought iron gates and white rail fences, I already know where it is."

She blushed. "That would be it."

"Okay, then. I'll see you at one."

ALEX'S PALMS began to sweat as he neared Foxwood Farms. What was he doing here? Caitlin Kramer's horses were obviously way out of his league, and now that he really thought about it, so was she. He had no business pretending he could afford a horse from such a highbrow ranch. But he hadn't wanted to disappoint Hallie, and he figured the outing would do her good. If nothing else, she'd have a fun afternoon looking at all the horses, and then he would suggest they shop somewhere else.

Maybe Caitlin would point him in the direction of a horse breeder more within his budget. He grimaced, the thought just as sour in his mind as he knew the words would taste in his mouth. It wasn't that he was trying to keep up with the Joneses. It was more a matter of wishing it was within his power to give Hallie whatever she wanted. He didn't want to spoil her. He just wanted to shower her with love and anything that would make her happy.

"Daddy, look!" In her excitement, Hallie called him by the term of endearment she'd claimed to have outgrown some time ago. "Look at all the colts!" She pointed out the window at the mares and foals, grazing in a postcard-perfect expanse of green grass behind white fencing. Some of the foals played and bucked. Others nursed or nibbled grass alongside the mares, fuzzy tails flicking.

The sight brought back memories of his palomino mare, Goldie, and the buckskin colt she'd had the summer he was thirteen. He'd had to sell it when he and his mother moved to Denver.

Alex stopped in front of the set of wrought iron, electronic gates. He pressed the security buzzer and spoke to Caitlin through the speaker, then pulled his truck through the gates as they whirred open. Hallie was out of the pickup before it had even come to a complete stop.

Caitlin greeted them from the front porch. "Hi. Are you ready to look at some horses, Hallie?"

"You bet! Your foals are so cute."

"Thanks. We can take a closer look at them, too, if you want."

"All right." Hallie dogged Caitlin's heels as she made her way toward the paddocks, leaning heavily on her cane.

Suddenly, it occurred to Alex that maybe she was more exhausted from her physical therapy than she wanted to admit. But then, he supposed she would've had Dillon show them around if that were so.

She led them on a mini tour of the ranch, driving them in a golf cart. "This is about the only motorized thing I've been behind the wheel of lately," she said. "But I suppose it's a start." After petting the foals, they went with her to the main barn. "Want to meet Red Fire and Black Knight?" she asked.

"Sure." Hallie nodded, her ponytail bobbing.

Alex was in awe of the entire setup. Everywhere he looked were signs of immense wealth. Stable hands, exercise riders…high-dollar equipment of every sort imaginable, including a trio of electronic hot walkers outside the barn. He followed Hallie and Caitlin into the spacious barn. On either side of the aisle were rows of stalls with adjoining paddocks. Caitlin led them to one near the center of the building. Inside stood a huge black horse, probably a good sixteen and a half hands high, Alex guessed.

"This is Black Knight," Caitlin said. "He's eight." She stroked the gelding's neck as he leaned over the stall door.

The big horse lowered his muzzle toward Hallie as she tentatively stepped closer and ran her fingertips over the star on his forehead. "He's huge!"

Caitlin chuckled. "Yes, he is—sixteen-point-three hands." She moved to the next stall and spoke to the chestnut inside.

While this one wasn't nearly as big as Black Knight, he was still a good size—about fifteen and a half hands. Alex definitely had something smaller in mind for Hallie.

"And this is Red Fire," Caitlin said, her affection for the horse obvious in her voice. She cradled his head in her hands as he nuzzled her. "I've had him since he was four. He was my first speed-event horse outside of the Welsh ponies I rode early on. He's seventeen…still in his prime."

Hallie stroked the chestnut's nose. "You're a pretty boy, aren't you?" she cooed.

"Actually, horses can reach their thirties," Caitlin said, "given the right care and a little luck."

"I know, I've been reading a lot," Hallie said.

"That's a good thing. Knowledge is power." She grinned, and Alex's heart raced.

God, she was beautiful. "So, how old were you when you got Red Fire?" he asked, hoping the question sounded casual, as though he were wondering if she'd been near Hallie's age.

"Not much younger than Hallie," she said. Her impish grin told him she was on to him. "I was ten, and I've had him for almost fourteen years. So that would make me twenty-four." She widened her eyes at him. "Not the child you thought I was."

He felt his face heat. "You are compared to my decrepit thirty."

She laughed. "Hardly."

Then she turned to Hallie as though realizing she was flirting with him in front of his daughter. No. It was more than that. Her entire attitude and body posture suddenly changed, as though she'd become abruptly aware of…what?

"So where are the horses that are for sale?" Hallie asked.

"We've got some in the barn, some out on pasture," Caitlin said. She hesitated, and Alex frowned. Maybe she was finally realizing her horses were out of his price range. The thought irritated him.

"You can show us the horses," he said. "I might not have enough to buy something for six figures, but I am capable of paying for a quality animal for my daughter." *He hoped.* Lord, what if he'd just put his foot in his mouth but good? If she called his bluff...

He kept his poker face in place. To his annoyance, Caitlin seemed amused.

"I wasn't implying anything to the contrary," she said. "I was thinking that Red Fire is just standing here going to waste. I mean, he gets exercised regularly, but he's happiest performing in the arena, aren't you, boy?" She cupped the gelding's jaw between her hands and planted a kiss on his muzzle.

Alex shivered. Her hands looked so soft. She had slim, delicate fingers and creamy skin, and somehow his mind was on something else, not horses.

"You mean you'd sell him?" Hallie asked eagerly.

"No, I couldn't part with him," Caitlin said. "But I could loan him to you."

"Really?" Hallie's eyes were round with anticipation.

"If it's all right with your dad."

"Whoa, hold on." Alex held up his hand, glancing at the horse. "He's awfully big."

"Dad, he's *perfect*." Hallie bobbed up and down, waving her arms.

He hadn't seen her this enthusiastic, this happy in ages. He wavered.

"He's fifteen-two," Caitlin said. "Smaller than any other horse on this ranch."

"I'm familiar with how to measure a horse," Alex said, feeling like a fool for not realizing the Kramers would only have big horses. He was used to quarter horses, which averaged about fifteen hands.

"Sorry." She smirked.

"And fifteen-two is tall," he went on.

Caitlin shrugged. "I guess I'm used to sixteen-plus jumpers."

"He's perfect, Dad," Hallie repeated, eyes sparkling. She reached once more to stroke the chestnut's blaze. "And he's already trained for barrel racing."

"Size is not the point anyway," Caitlin said. "Red Fire is gentle and trustworthy. Bombproof. Child-proof." She shrugged. "He'd never purposely do anything to hurt his rider."

"I was thinking more along the lines of *short* and gentle."

"I don't want a *pony*," Hallie said.

"There are plenty of good horses under fifteen hands, Hal," Alex replied. But he felt himself weakening, even as he tried to stand firm. He'd do just about anything to keep her happy.

"I think I know a way to make you feel better about this," Caitlin said. She motioned. "Come on. I'll show you something."

She led them to the sprawling, ranch-style house that stood centered on emerald-green landscaped grounds, with a marble fountain in front and creatively sculpted hedges. A stone walkway led to a massive, brick-trimmed porch. The front door opened before they mounted the stairs.

The dark-haired woman he'd seen that day at Pearl's Diner flashed a welcome smile at him and Hallie. "Hello, there," she said. "I see you made it over to visit our horses." She held out her hand. "Caitlin and Dillon have told us all about you."

"Alex, meet my mother, Evelyn. Mom, Alex Hunter and his daughter, Hallie."

"Your mother? Whoa." Alex flashed Evelyn a grin, unable to stop himself. "I thought you were Caitlin's sister."

Her laugh was full and genuine. "Oh, I like him already." She winked at her daughter. "Come in, come in. Hallie, how are you, dear?" Evelyn held the door wide, welcoming them into a foyer that could've swallowed his and Hallie's living room.

Alex tried not to stare, but he couldn't help taking in the curved, sweeping staircase that dominated the far end. Photos of jumping horses lined the wall along it, and at the top of the staircase, overlooking the foyer, was a portrait of a young, blue-eyed woman and an elegant steel-dust-gray Thoroughbred.

Caitlin caught him staring. "That's Gran," she said, indicating the portrait, "and her all-time favorite show jumper, Iron Sword."

"If your grandmother looks that young," Alex said, "then I assume that's the Fountain of Youth I saw in the yard."

She laughed. "It's Gran when she was fifteen."

"Speaking of which, I'm off to meet her for lunch and to look at a stallion," Evelyn said, glancing at her watch. She kissed Caitlin firmly on the cheek. "I'll see you later, honey. Bye, Hallie. It was nice to meet you, and you, too, Alex."

"Likewise." He nodded, but Hallie was too enthralled by her surroundings to answer.

"Wow!" She spun in a circle, looking up at the vast ceiling...the chandelier overhead. "Why do you live in that old farm when you could live here?"

"Hallie!" Alex felt his face warm, but Caitlin only laughed.

"I have my reasons. Come on, let me show you why I brought you in here." Alex followed her across a floor polished to such a high shine it looked wet.

Caitlin opened a set of double oak doors, and they stepped into a sitting room, a den…a library?

He had no idea what the proper term would be. But bookshelves lined two walls, and over a marble fireplace in the third wall hung yet another portrait of a Thoroughbred. Trophies stood displayed on the mantel, the bookshelves and in three glass-fronted cabinets, representing jumping and Lord knew what other equestrian events. They ranged in size from modest to monstrous. And ribbons decorated yet another display case in shades of red, blue and violet.

Made the team-penning trophy buckle he'd won as a kid look puny.

From a drawer in a massive oak desk, Caitlin pulled out a scrapbook and sank onto a leather sofa. "Have a seat." She indicated the couch on either side of her, then spread the book open on her lap. Alex sat beside her, fully aware of how close she was. She smelled wonderful, her skin scented with something subtle and sweet. He focused on the scrapbook.

On the first page was an eight-by-ten photo of a girl on a chestnut horse. "This is me and Red Fire at our first show. I was ten and he was four." Caitlin tapped the yellow medallion-shaped ribbon on the opposite page. "We took third place in pole bending, and had a pretty darned fast time going on the barrels until I knocked one over." She grimaced. "Five-second penalty."

Hallie squirmed with barely contained excitement. "That is so awesome."

Caitlin turned the page. "This is us at our second show. That time we took home two blues and a red. Poles, barrels and scurry jump." She continued to flip through the scrapbook, and Alex couldn't help but be impressed by the sequence of photos, showing Caitlin and her gelding from the time she was ten until she was sixteen, when she gave up barrel racing for jumping.

She nodded toward the display case. "Some of our trophies are in those cases. So, you see—" Caitlin looked at him as she closed the scrapbook "—Red Fire is completely safe for a kid to ride. Now do you feel better?" The impish look in her eyes set his blood on fire.

Acutely aware that his knee was touching hers beneath the scrapbook, Alex shifted and cleared his throat. "I'm not sure yet."

Caitlin studied him for a moment. "What would you say to letting Hallie try him out in the arena?"

"I say yes!" Hallie bounced in place on the couch.

"I don't know." Alex looked at his daughter, her eyes lit up. If something so simple as a horse could make such a difference to Hallie, then who was he to say no? "All right." But he cut Hallie off mid-squeal. "On one condition. You wear proper safety equipment and you keep the horse at a walk." He looked at Caitlin. "You do have a helmet for her?"

"I sure do. And boots," she added. "We keep a few pairs on hand in various sizes for guests, so we ought to have something that will fit." She picked up her cane and rose from the couch.

Alex picked up the scrapbook. "Allow me." He put it away in the desk drawer, then followed Caitlin outside. Hallie skipped ahead of them.

From the tack room's corner cabinet, Caitlin took two pairs of riding boots, gauging Hallie's feet. "What size shoe do you wear?" Hallie told her, and she held out one pair of the shiny black boots. "Go ahead and try them while I get you a helmet."

Once Hallie had her boots, Alex carried an English saddle from the room while the girl helped Caitlin haul tack and grooming tools toward Red Fire's stall. He started to offer to catch the gelding, but Caitlin managed on her own, leaning the cane against the wall of the box stall while she haltered the well-mannered gelding. Impressed by the deft way she handled the horse in spite of her injuries, Alex watched as Caitlin led the horse into the aisle and put him in cross ties.

A short time later, she had him saddled and, leaning on her cane, led him from the barn. Alex fought the urge to take the horse's lead from her. Obviously, she was capable. He relaxed, taken with Red Fire's calm nature. When they reached the arena, Alex opened the gate for Caitlin, and the three of them stepped inside with the horse. He closed the gate and latched it.

"Would you mind if I warm him up before Hallie rides?"

"Not at all." She handed him the reins. "I was just about to suggest that. Not that he needs it, but I think it'll make you feel more at ease."

Alex eyed the small hunk of leather that passed for a saddle. "I've never ridden English before." He shot her a grin, tugging his cowboy hat down tight. "Actually, it's been quite a while since I've been on a horse at all."

"You know what they say," Caitlin said. "Like riding a bike." She gauged the length of his leg and adjusted the stirrup irons. "That ought to be about right. Give it a try."

Used to having a saddle horn to grip for mounting, Alex placed one hand awkwardly on the pommel and one on the cantle, then swung quickly onto Red Fire's back. The gelding stood obediently still, which was a good thing, since Alex very nearly lost his balance. He grinned sheepishly, adjusting the reins. "Feels almost like riding bareback, but with stirrups."

Caitlin laughed softly, and again, the sound teased his libido. "I'm sorry. I don't own a western saddle anymore. But Red Fire will ride English or western, so if you decide you like him, you can always get Hallie a western saddle. She'll need one to do gymkhana."

"One step at a time." Using his knees and lower legs, Alex signaled Red Fire to move forward. Caitlin was right. Within minutes, he felt comfortable on the gelding, and even the strange saddle wasn't so bad once he got used to it. He put the chestnut through his paces—walking, trotting and loping in circles and figure eights.

"Hurry up, Dad!" Hallie called out impatiently. "I want a turn."

He brought the horse to a halt in front of them, then swung down. "He's really nice."

"Told you." Caitlin smirked, readjusting the stirrups for Hallie.

Alex fought the urge to help his daughter into the saddle. He wanted to hold on to her, to walk beside her like he'd once done when she was very little and he'd taken her for a pony ride at a local carnival.

"Want a leg up?" Caitlin asked as Hallie tried awkwardly to place her foot into the stirrup.

"Sure."

Caitlin handed him her cane, then made a footrest by lacing her fingers together, palms up, standing beside Red Fire. Her left hand seemed to perform a bit awkwardly, Alex noticed, and she winced as Hallie stepped into her hands and used them to hoist herself onto the gelding's back. For a split second, he saw the weakness in Caitlin's left arm, but she hid it quickly.

"There you go." She helped Hallie get her other foot properly in the iron, making sure the stirrups were indeed the right length, then gave her a few instructions on how to guide and cue the horse.

She stepped back. "He's all yours."

Alex held his breath and watched his daughter take the big horse in a slow circle around the perimeter of the arena. Her face literally glowed, and her eyes held a spark he hadn't seen in them in a long while.

"She looks good up there," Caitlin said, standing beside him.

"Yes, she does." His worries began to fade and he smiled as he watched his little girl ride. She was a natural. She handled Red Fire like she'd been doing it all her life.

"Take him in a figure eight," Caitlin called. "That's it."

"Can I trot him, Dad?" Hallie called after a few minutes.

He started to say no. But he knew he'd been overprotective, and that the horse could be trusted. "Okay, but take it easy."

"Just squeeze him gently with your calves," Caitlin called out. "Don't kick him."

Hallie tried, but couldn't quite get the hang of it until Caitlin walked over and gave her additional instructions. Soon, Hallie had Red Fire trotting in a circle. She bobbed like a sack of potatoes on the horse's back.

"I'll have to teach her to post a trot," Caitlin said. "I'll have to do it from the ground, unfortunately."

Their eyes met, and Alex watched a shadow pass over her face.

"You can't ride yet, huh?"

"No, not yet." She kept a watchful eye on Hallie, avoiding his gaze. "I'm not sure I'll ever be able to. Guess you'd better get her that western saddle if you're going to let her keep riding. Maybe find someone to give her lessons."

"Yeah, I guess I'd better." He studied her profile. "Of course, I can't say as I'm going to be the best at picking out a saddle that fits properly. It's been a long time since I've owned a horse."

"Walk him now," Caitlin called out to Hallie.

He waited. "Would you go with me?"

She shifted, leaning heavily on the cane. "I don't know."

"I want to make sure I don't choose one that gives your horse saddle sores." It was also the perfect excuse to spend more time with her. "I'd appreciate your help."

She hesitated. "I suppose I can, then. The feed store sells new and used tack, but they're closed for the day and won't open back up until Monday. They might have something, or we can try an auction.

They hold one at the sale barn the third Saturday of every month, which is next weekend."

"Sounds good," he said. "Either way. Maybe you can give her riding lessons."

She avoided his gaze. "I told you I can't."

"I understand you can't get on the horse and actually show her how to ride. But you can instruct her from the ground…just like you're doing now."

She glanced at him. "That's true, but it's not the same. She needs someone who can do it all. Who can demonstrate what they're teaching her."

"Don't look at me," he said. "As you saw, I'm pretty rusty. You can teach her a lot more than I can."

"I don't think so, Alex." She fell silent.

They watched Hallie ride until Alex realized Caitlin looked tired. "That's enough for today, Hallie," he called out. "You don't want to wear poor Red Fire out on your first ride."

"Just one more circle?" Hallie begged.

"It's all right," Caitlin said. "I'm fine."

But she didn't look fine when they headed back to the barn to unsaddle the gelding. Alex did it for her, and showed Hallie how to brush the horse down. How to clean his hooves out with a hoof pick.

"Looks like you remember some of the important parts of owning a horse," Caitlin said, making an effort to hide the fact that she was in discomfort, if not pain.

"Yeah, well, as you said. It's sort of like riding a bicycle." He led Red Fire toward his stall.

"I can take him," Caitlin said.

"Let me," Hallie begged.

Alex met Caitlin's gaze, grateful his daughter had given her the perfect out. Saved Caitlin's pride.

"Sure," Caitlin said. "You might as well get used to him if you're going to be using him for a while."

"I wish Foxwood Farms was next door to our place," Hallie said. "I doubt if Dad will let me ride my bike over here, even though it's only a couple of miles." She glared accusingly at him.

"You won't have to come here," Caitlin said. "I told you I'd loan him to you."

Hallie stared blankly at her for a moment, then sucked in her breath. "You mean you're going to bring him to our house?"

"Sure, as soon as your dad prepares a place to keep him. Meantime, he can stay with Silver Fox."

"Cool!"

"Hang on," Alex said. "I haven't said yes yet."

Hallie's face fell. "But, Dad, Red Fire's great! I love him. Pleeeze?" She clasped her folded hands in a begging motion.

"It really is okay with me," Caitlin said. "Truly."

What the heck.

"Well, if you're sure."

"Ye-es!" Hallie jumped in the air, pumping one fist triumphantly. "When can we get him?"

"Dillon's out with Dad today," Caitlin said. "But I'm sure tomorrow will be fine. He'll trailer him over."

"All right!" Hallie hurried back to Red Fire's stall. "Hear that, boy? You're going to come live with Silver Fox and be my horse."

"Hallie," Alex cautioned. "We're only borrowing him." He frowned at her. "Where are your manners?"

"Sorry." She smiled. "Thanks, Caitlin."

"You're more than welcome. I'm sure Silver Fox will enjoy the company."

"Come on, Hallie. We've taken up enough of Caitlin's time. Let's go home."

"O-o-h!" With a final pat to Red Fire's neck, she reluctantly left the stall and headed out to the truck.

"Need a ride home?" Alex asked. He knew he shouldn't. Caitlin's family would see her safely back later. He should keep his time with her to a minimum. Strictly for Hallie's benefit.

But a part of him ached for some benefits of his own. She was a beautiful and fascinating woman.

Her blue eyes mesmerized him as he waited for an answer. Even handling Red Fire on the ground, it was easy to imagine how graceful Caitlin must be in the saddle.

"We're going that way anyway," he said. "I bet it

wouldn't take more than a quarter's worth of gas to make the extra hundred yards to your place."

She laughed. "At the price of gas, it might be more like a dollar. But sure, if you don't mind that'd be great. Just let me leave a note for Mom up at the house."

"I'll walk you." She looked increasingly shaky and tired.

But Caitlin showed him what tough stuff she was made of she used her cane and doggedly walked the distance. He waved aside her invitation to come in, instead waiting on the porch with Hallie.

"Thanks, Dad," Hallie said once Caitlin was out of earshot.

He looked at her, surprised. "For what?"

"For treating me like my age instead of my shoe size."

He grimaced. "Have I been that bad?"

"The worst."

"I'm sorry." He reached out to caress her cheek. "I'll try to do better."

She nodded. "You're off to a good start. Red Fire is awesome."

He laughed. "Yes, he is."

And so was Caitlin Kramer. He'd have to curb his desire. He had more important things to focus on. Like looking after Hallie, making sure she got better.

She was the most important thing in his life, and he'd do well to remember that.

CHAPTER FIVE

CAITLIN HAD BARELY closed the door behind her after Alex dropped her off, when the phone rang. She moved as quickly as she could to answer it, dodging Spike as the dog jumped straight into the air to greet her, as if his legs were made of pogo springs.

"Hello?"

"Hi. How's it going?"

"Hey, Shauna. I'm doing okay." Caitlin sank onto the couch, welcoming the chance to rest.

"I was wondering if you were free tonight," Shauna asked.

"No, I'm going out dancing," Caitlin said dryly. "Then after that, I think I'll run a marathon."

"Hey, stop that. You'll be dancing before you know it."

With effort, Caitlin shrugged off the dark thoughts that threatened to send her mood into a downward spiral. "I don't know about that, but what did you have in mind?"

"Don't sound so suspicious. I'm not planning

anything as terrible as taking you out and forcing you to socialize." She laughed. "I've got a three-day weekend. I thought I could bring over some DVDs and pizza and we can have a movie night."

"I don't know, Shauna. I'm pretty tired."

"Well then how about tomorrow night? It'll be fun and, if you get tired early, fall asleep. I won't mind. I'll watch Johnny Depp by myself and eat your share of the pizza."

Caitlin couldn't help but laugh. "Johnny Depp, huh? Okay. Throw in some butter-free popcorn and you've got a deal." Pizza was her one junk food indulgence, though she rarely ate it, and she did have a weakness for sexy pirates. "Tell you what—bring your pj's and we'll have a slumber party." She hated to admit it, but she'd found the house strangely quiet last night. "I've got an extra bedroom if you don't mind bringing a sleeping bag, since there's no furniture in it yet. Or you can crash in my room and I'll sleep on the couch."

"Don't be ridiculous. You need your bed. Is seven-thirty okay?"

"Perfect." They said their goodbyes and Caitlin hung up. She felt ashamed that after the accident she'd felt like hiding from everyone, including her best friend. A girls' night in might allow her to forget that things weren't normal in her life.

She lay on the couch and slept for an hour. When

she woke up, she freshened up in the bathroom, then went outside to feed Silver Fox. To her relief, Hallie was nowhere in sight. Not that she didn't like the girl, but she needed some time alone. Being by herself helped her sort out her thoughts.

In the barn, she saw the three bales of hay Alex had stacked on the floor for her. She felt both gratitude and resentment, not toward him but her body for being unable to function properly. She fed Fox, then stood leaning on the fence outside. The red Chevy truck caught her attention. Dillon had parked it in the driveway between the house and barn, and the keys were on a peg near the back door in the kitchen.

God, she was itching to drive it. She missed being behind the wheel so much. She looked from the Chevy to the horizon where the evening sun still burned. The pasture, tall with grass turned gold by the late summer heat, stretched out beyond the barn and paddock. The farm sat on fifteen acres, and the Realtor she'd leased from had assured her she was welcome to use the entire property. At the time, she hadn't paid much attention to details since all she cared about was the house and the privacy.

Funny how meeting Alex Hunter and his daughter had quickly swayed her from self-seclusion. And she couldn't explain why. Caitlin forced herself to stop thinking about the man's gorgeous dark eyes and tried to recall what the Realtor had said about the fence around the pasture. The section close to the house and barn was split rail, but she doubted the entire acreage was fenced that way. Now that she planned to bring Red Fire out, it might be nice to use the pasture and give the two horses a place to graze and stretch their legs. Lord knew Fox wasn't getting the exercise he was used to.

Her Chevy. She really hadn't planned on trying to drive it this soon. But she had a couple of hours of daylight left. Surely she could at least manage to steer the truck through the pasture and have a look at the fence. She'd noticed faint tire tracks in the grass beyond the barn where someone had once driven out into the field. There was probably an old dirt lane beneath the overgrowth.

In a flash, she saw the out-of-control SUV heading her way—as clear as it had been on the highway that night. *Shit!* She had to stop doing that to herself. She had to drive again.

She could go as slow as she needed to, and if she got dizzy, she could simply step on the brake and stop without fear of hitting anything or anyone.

It would be a long walk back to the house if she got the truck stuck out in the field or was unable to maneuver it after all. But if she didn't try, she'd never know.

Caitlin retrieved the keys and called to Spike. The terrier leaped into the pickup, stubby tail wagging, front feet on the steering wheel. "Unless you're planning to drive, Spike, you'd better scoot over." Then again, maybe she ought to let the dog drive, she thought dryly, nudging him over as she eased behind the wheel. Her hip ached, and so did her back. She'd overexerted herself today, and she knew it, but she couldn't resist taking her new pickup for a spin. Her cane on the floorboard, Caitlin turned the key in the ignition and shifted into drive.

It felt odd to be behind the wheel again. She'd been afraid that the first time she drove she might have flashbacks to the night of the accident, but all she felt was exhilaration as the truck rolled along at a tame ten miles an hour. She refused to think about the times she'd taken the Jag out late at night on deserted highways and cut loose.

The distance to the stock gate wasn't far, yet she felt a sense of accomplishment as she parked the truck to get out and open the gate. A moment later she was on her way, steering along the dirt trail, pushing the truck to twenty. Not exactly racing, but it felt fast to her. A little light-headed, her palms began to sweat. Veering too close to the edge of the track the truck hit a fist-size rock in the tall grass. She gasped as the wheel slipped from her grip, and she slammed on the brake. Spike pitched forward onto the floor.

"Whoa. Sorry, buddy. Oh, Spike." Caitlin put the

truck in Park and reached over to comfort the terrier. He bounded into her arms, not one bit hurt, but willing to take full advantage of her sympathy. He licked her face, eating up every bit of her attention.

She took a steadying breath. "Okay, let's try again." *Maybe she ought to get Spike a doggy car seat.*

The remainder of her drive went without incident, and by the time she inspected the pasture fence—Spike bounding along beside her—she felt a sense of accomplishment. Her hands shook, and her knees were a bit like overcooked spaghetti, but she'd done it.

Caitlin examined the fence. It was barbed wire, just as she'd suspected. The four-strand wire was in good shape, stretched tight between sturdy wooden posts. Great for cattle, not for horses. There was no way she'd risk turning her geldings out in that. She'd have Dillon come out with one of the stable hands and run an electric wire along the perimeter. The horses were familiar with electric fencing and knew not to test it. Caitlin had taken a jolt or two off an electric fence herself and, while no fun, it wasn't dangerous. Barbed wire, on the other hand, was cruel.

Back in the truck, Caitlin made a three-point turn and headed toward the barn. It was only after she parked that she smelled a faint odor of something burning. Sniffing, she looked around, worried about fire. It had been pretty dry this year, with not nearly as much rain as usual. She hoped no one was foolishly burning weeds. But it smelled more like something was melting…like plastic. Frowning, Caitlin walked around the pickup and saw a wisp of smoke curling out from beneath her wheel wells. *Good grief!* Had her engine overheated?

Not even knowing what to look for, she nevertheless bent and peered beneath the truck, and let out a gasp. A huge wad of orange baling twine was wrapped around a long, pipelike thing. The nylon material was apparently hot enough to melt. Phew! Caitlin waved her hand in front of her nose, beginning to panic. Would the truck catch fire? It didn't seem likely, but then, she knew nothing about cars. She hated to call the fire department for what might turn out to be a false alarm. But she didn't want her Chevy to erupt into flames.

Alex.

Cane in hand, fighting the way her brain seemed to pitch her off balance after having bent under the truck, Caitlin made her way as quickly as she could to the house. But she hesitated with her hand on the cordless. She hated to bother the man…maybe she should call Dillon. Right. He'd give her an ass-chewing for having driven the Chevy. Damn!

She drummed her fingers against the end table.

Her father would be just as upset, if not more so. How on earth had twine gotten tangled up like that? She doubted her auto club service covered such an unusual situation.

Caitlin jumped as the phone rang beside her. "Hello?"

"Caitlin? It's Alex."

"Alex!" Her skin tingled at the sound of his husky voice.

"Is everything okay with you? Your brother called. He was worried because he couldn't reach you. Said he was going to drive out."

Caitlin counted to ten. "Dillon's a little overprotective. I'm sorry he bothered you."

"It's no bother. I'm glad everything's okay." He paused. "Are you sure nothing's wrong? You sound kind of funny."

She twisted a piece of her hair around one finger. "It's nothing really. I've just had a little incident. It's stupid."

"What?"

"I don't want to impose on you."

"Caitlin, I'm right across the road. What do you need?"

Feeling like a moron, she explained about the baling twine. "But you don't have to come over, really. I was about to call my brother anyway."

"If your truck is smoking it could be dangerous.

Dillon was on his way from Aspen, so it's going to take him a while. I'll be right over."

He hung up before she could protest. Caitlin put the cordless back on its base, relieved but also irritated. She couldn't even be away from the phone for a little while without her family thinking she'd fallen and died. As soon as the thought was out, she felt guilty. She *had* come close to dying. Could she blame them? Besides, she *had* gotten into trouble and *did* need help right now. That is what irritated her the most.

Outside, she spotted Alex striding across the road toward her. He greeted her, then bent to peer under the truck.

"Wow." He straightened. "That twine's wrapped all around your driveshaft at the carrier bearing. It's tangled inside your U-joint and everything."

She blinked. "Could you please speak English?"

"Basically, you've got a real mess there. How in the world did it happen?"

"I don't know. Like I said, I drove out to inspect the fence." She shrugged. "I guess the twine must've been hidden in the grass and weeds."

"Well it must be an awfully long piece. Several lengths tied together, in fact. Somebody must've been using the string for a marker of some sort. Maybe to mark off a potential fence line."

"Will it catch on fire?" Caitlin wrinkled her nose

at the acrid smell. But the smoke seemed to have dissipated.

"I don't think so. Still, the fumes from your gas tank are not exactly something to ignore."

Panic seized her. "My God. I'd better call the fire department."

"There's no need for that. I really don't think it's going to burst into flames. But we need to get that twine off there." He lowered himself to the ground, ready to crawl under the truck.

"You don't have to do that," Caitlin protested. "You'll ruin your clothes. Dillon will be here sooner or later." She tried not to stare at his faded jeans and what they couldn't hide from her imagination. Tried not to picture Alex with his shirt off.

He gave her a crooked grin. "It's a T-shirt and jeans. They'll wash." With that, he slid beneath the truck like an ace mechanic, disappearing from view.

Caitlin crouched awkwardly to watch as Alex took a large folding knife from his pocket and began to saw patiently at the wad of twine. "Damn, that's really melted on there." He grimaced. "It'll take a while to get off."

"Really, Alex, let me call a tow truck or something."

"I don't mind. Don't worry about it."

She glanced over at his house. "Where's Hallie?"

"In her room. I think she's tired from our outing."

She heard the smile in his voice even though she didn't have a clear view of his face. "I haven't seen her so excited since I don't know when. I sure appreciate your letting her ride Red Fire."

"No problem." Caitlin relaxed as they talked, happy she could do something nice for the girl.

An hour later Dillon pulled his silver Ford dually into her driveway. He got out and hurried toward her.

"Caitlin, my God, where have you been? I've tried and tried to call you. I asked Alex to come over and check on you. Where the hell is he?"

"Right here." A pair of cowboy boots appeared beneath the pickup's bed as Alex scooted out from under the Chevy and stood, his hands black with grease. Smudges of grease and grime marked his face and the front of his T-shirt. He held a wad of mangled twine that resembled a nest spun by some berserk bird.

Dillon's face reddened. "Alex. I didn't see you under there." He frowned. "What were you doing?"

"Cutting this baling twine off your sister's driveshaft."

"What? How the hell did that happen?" He scowled at Caitlin. "You drove."

She crossed her arms. "Can we please discuss this later?"

He took a step forward, gesturing vehemently. "What were you thinking? Where'd you go? Do you realize how dangerous it is to drive in your condition?"

Caitlin's temper flared. "I'm not a child, Dillon, and I'm not stupid. I only drove in the pasture."

"Oh, well then that's okay," he said sarcastically. "Hell, if anything went wrong you'd be sitting out there in the middle of nowhere for God knows how long until someone found you."

"Fifteen acres is hardly the middle of nowhere," she shot back. "You're out of line."

"Out of line?" He pointed at his chest. "I'm out of line? I think you'd better take a look at yourself, Cate. I'm beginning to see why Mom and Dad didn't want you to move out here in the first place."

Caitlin's mouth gaped. "Dillon!" She struggled to get a grip on her anger, knowing her face must be beet-red, embarrassed that Alex should witness such a personal argument.

"No, I mean it. Gran told you to keep your cell phone with you at all times, and what do you do? Leave it at home, as usual." He gestured toward the house. "Let me guess. It's sitting on the kitchen table, am I right? Didn't you learn anything after the crash?"

Light-headed—stunned that her brother would be so cruel—hurt threatened to overwhelm her. But before she could respond, Alex stepped between her and Dillon.

"That's enough," he said firmly. His dark eyes looked furious as he stood toe to toe with Dillon, equally as tall.

"This doesn't concern you," Dillon said.

"That's where you're wrong." Alex's hand was a fist at his side, squeezing the wad of twine. "If memory serves me right, you told me you were happy to have someone like me around to keep an eye on your sister."

Caitlin scowled at Dillon. "You told him that? I don't need a damned babysitter!" Furious, she glared at the two of them. "You can both just butt out."

She spun on her heel and headed for the house.

HALLIE SAT in her room, staring out the window. She'd heard her dad on the telephone with Caitlin and knew he'd gone over to help with something to do with Caitlin's pickup. Normally, she would've gone with him.

But in spite of the fun she'd had earlier that day, her spirits were sinking as dusk turned the sky gray. Darkness often brought on depression since Melissa's death. Sometimes she wondered if her dad should've let their doctor put her on antidepressants. But he seemed to think they weren't something to give a kid. He treated her like a baby.

She wished he'd lighten up. He'd lose it if he ever found out how she coped when she felt out of control. After Melissa died she'd lost control of everything.

A tear slid down her cheek and she wiped it away.

She couldn't stop those boys from shooting Melissa. She'd stood there, frozen with fear, too shocked to even scream. She could barely remember what had happened after Melissa fell to the ground. Had absolutely no memory of riding to the hospital with her father.

But she did recall the way her friends had gathered around her once she'd gone back to school. And not just friends. A lot of the kids had been fascinated by what had happened to her cousin. They'd made her sick. She skipped classes, and once, hadn't gone to school at all. Instead, she'd spent the day with Alicia and Courtney, who'd become her closest friends after Melissa had… She'd forged her dad's name on a written excuse, and he'd never known.

Not part of the popular crowd at school, Alicia and Courtney were much like her in that respect. And like her, they did their best to wear the right clothes and act cool, trying to fit in. Alicia and Courtney were cute, though. She was a good ten pounds heavier than either of them. So she was surprised when they'd gone to Alicia's house while her parents were at work and spread out a bunch of snacks in Alicia's bedroom and proceeded to pig out.

And that was when she'd discovered how her friends kept their weight down.

When they'd told her about binging and purging, she'd been disgusted. It sounded so gross. But the more she thought about it, the more it made her curious to try it. Just once. Her emotions out of control, hating the world, Hallie had dug in with her friends—chocolate bars, nacho cheese and chips, mint-chocolate ice cream. They'd downed cans of pop and then took turns in the bathroom.

Alicia had explained how easy it was to take control of your body. To make your stomach give up all the food that would make you fat. Courtney had encouraged her, and had even offered to stay with her by the toilet bowl. She'd refused. She wasn't even sure she could do what they'd said. It took her twenty minutes. When it was over, she'd stood shaking beside the basin, feeling nothing but relief and peace.

It had taken some practice before she got the hang of purging. And it was Courtney who'd shown her how to use a spoon instead of her fingers, to keep from getting a callus on her knuckles. At first she'd purged only once in a while. But then she did it more and more. It helped her keep her weight at an average level, even though she ate whatever she wanted. And it was the only time she felt in control. The only thing in her life she had control over.

As much as she'd wanted a horse, when her father had told her they were moving to Deer Creek, she'd been devastated to leave Alicia and Courtney. To start classes at a new school. But they'd promised to come visit her. And when they did, they'd be glad to know she hadn't made any new best friends at Deer Creek Middle School. As a matter of fact, the more she binged and purged, the more she relished keeping her actions a secret. Keeping to herself.

Courtney had given her a very special present on the day they'd come over to say goodbye. One Hallie had kept hidden from her father.

She moved to the closet and stood on tiptoe to reach the top shelf. Moving aside a purse and some stuffed animals, she took down a shoebox. On her bed, she removed the lid and took out the pottery bowl Courtney had made for her. It was the size of a large soup bowl.

Is it really big enough? she'd asked. Courtney had assured her it was. Some girls even used a purging cup. Of course, if she really planned on a solid binge, she'd have to use the toilet. Or a trash can. Or the bushes.

But for privacy in her own room, the bowl would suffice. Courtney had painted things on it. A girl's face with tears running down her cheeks and a few words from a poem she'd written to express her own feelings about binging and purging. Control. Relief. Peace.

Her dad would likely be at Caitlin's for some time yet and, knowing she could easily feign sleep if he knocked at her door, Hallie sat in her darkening bedroom with the lights off. She placed the purging bowl on the table beside her lamp and the latest Saddle Club book. Then she went to her dresser and pulled out the bag of cookies she'd hidden.

Sitting on the bed, letting her mind wander, she began to eat.

CHAPTER SIX

CAITLIN IGNORED Dillon's knock, but it did no good. He opened the door and stuck his head inside. "Cate," he called. "Can I come in?"

She started to refuse. She was mad as hell, not to mention hurt. She glared at him from the couch. "Do I have a choice?"

He looked genuinely remorseful as he stepped inside and closed the door behind him. "I'm sorry, Cate. I didn't mean what I said." He sat on the edge of the sofa beside her.

"Yes, you did."

He sighed. "Okay, I meant the part about you keeping your cell phone on hand. But I didn't mean what I said about the crash. Damn it, I'm an ass when I lose my temper."

"Yes, you are." She softened as she saw the concern her brother felt for her clearly reflected in his eyes. "But I love you anyway. Apology accepted."

"Just promise me you won't try driving again any time soon."

"Dillon." She stared at him. "I can't make you a promise I don't know if I'll be able to keep." She turned her hands up in frustration. "I have to try things. Otherwise, how am I ever going to make any progress?"

"That's fine. But at least wait until someone else is with you. Call me to go for a drive across the pasture with you. Or…"

"Or Alex Hunter?" She raised her eyebrow, taking pleasure in watching her brother squirm.

"Hey, I know you don't need a babysitter. But I worry. Can you blame me?"

"I guess not," she admitted grudgingly.

"And yes, I asked Alex to keep an eye on you. I just want to make sure you're safe here alone."

"I'm fine. Quit being such a mother hen."

"I'll try." He stood. "Well, if you're sure you're all right. Dad and I brought a couple of mares home today. I need to get back to the ranch."

The mention of hauling horses made her think of Red Fire. "Can I ask you a favor?"

"Sure. Anything."

"Can you bring Red Fire over tomorrow?"

Now it was Dillon's turn to raise an eyebrow. "What, first you don't even want Silver Fox here, and now you want Red Fire, too?"

"Not for me. I promised Hallie—Alex's daughter—she could use him." She shrugged. "No one rides him much these days."

He nodded. "Okay. When do you want me to come?"

"First thing in the morning? But not too early. I'm pooped."

"I'll bring him out about nine."

"Thanks."

"You're welcome." He stood. "But don't think I'm going soft. If I catch you driving alone, I'll come over here and pull out all your spark plug wires."

Caitlin tossed a pillow at him. Dillon dodged it, grinning. "See you in the morning."

She sat on the couch for a while after the sound of his truck faded into the distance. Now that she wasn't angry anymore, she felt a little guilty for snapping at Alex. After all, he'd only been trying to help.

She covered a yawn with her hand, then rose from the couch and made her way to bed.

ALEX STOOD in front of the bathroom sink, working hand cleaner into his palms and across the backs of his knuckles to get rid of the grease. The house seemed almost too quiet. Hallie was asleep in her room. He smirked at his reflection in the mirror as he washed the grease from his face as well.

Minutes later, he'd put on a clean T-shirt and jeans and sat in the living room drinking a can of Pepsi while he surfed channels with the TV's remote control. Damn, but he'd blown it. He'd had no right to interfere between Caitlin and her brother, but Dillon had come down so hard on her. What the hell was wrong with the guy? The hurt in Caitlin's eyes, inflicted by her brother's words, had made him furious. Made him want to punch the man.

Unable to focus on the television, Alex finished his Pepsi and went to bed.

He woke up thinking about Caitlin, wondering if Dillon would still bring Red Fire over for Hallie after the argument. He'd made a hasty exit last night after Caitlin stormed into the house, to keep from losing his temper. But not before watching Dillon knock on her door. He didn't see if she let her brother in.

After a quick shower, Alex made his way to the kitchen. Hallie was already up and raring to go. "Good morning, Hal. Did you sleep well?"

"I guess." She bounced around the kitchen, full of energy. "What time is Caitlin's brother bringing Red Fire? Did you ask her?"

"I don't know." He sidestepped her question, hating to disappoint her if the horse wasn't coming. "We'll have to see." But before he could even put the coffee on, he heard a vehicle outside.

Hallie ran to the window and let out a whoop. "He's here! Come on, Dad!"

"Hallie." He wanted to know if she'd had her breakfast. And he also needed a few minutes to pull himself together with a cup of java before he faced Caitlin. But Hallie was already out the door and across the road. With a sigh, Alex put the lid back on the coffee canister and grabbed his hat off the peg near the back door before heading outside.

Caitlin was in her yard, Spike running in circles, barking as the Ford truck pulled a matching horse trailer into the driveway. Dillon was behind the wheel. Last night, the two men had parted in an uncomfortable silence. Now Dillon nodded in greeting as he pulled the truck into place. Alex nodded back, then turned to Caitlin.

"Morning," he said.

"Good morning." She clipped the words out, letting him know she hadn't completely forgiven him. But her greeting for Hallie was all smiles and warmth.

"Hey, Hallie. Are you ready to say hello to Red Fire?"

"You bet. Can I ride him?"

Caitlin propped her cane against her body and blew into her cold hands. "We'll see. Of course, your dad is still going to have to get you a western saddle." She must have noticed the look of disappointment on Hallie's face, because she added, "Until then, you can use one of my English ones. I had Dillon bring the one you rode yesterday."

"Sweet!" Hallie rushed toward the horse trailer and climbed onto the running board to greet the horse through the bars of the window. "Hey, pretty boy. How're you?" She reached her fingers through to scratch his nose. Red Fire let out a loud whinny, and from the paddock nearby, Silver Fox screamed an answer.

"He's going to be a little excited by his new surroundings," Caitlin warned Hallie. "It's been a while since he traveled to gymkhanas, so we may want to give him some time to calm down before you ride him. But you can walk him and brush him."

"All right."

They followed Dillon around to the back of the horse trailer and watched as he unloaded the chestnut gelding. Red Fire came out of the trailer with the calm grace of a horse who'd been hauled numerous times, but he did perk his ears and let out another whinny to Silver Fox.

"I'll take him," Caitlin said, reaching to take the lead rope from Dillon.

"He could knock you down," Dillon said. "He's excited."

"I can handle him." Caitlin took the rope.

Alex admired her spunk, her determination to stand up for herself and fight the injuries the accident had left her with. He wasn't so sure he'd be as tough in her shoes, yet he could relate. He was determined to fight every inch of the way to get his daughter back to good health. And Caitlin had already contributed in a huge way toward Hallie's recovery. He owed her. He told himself that was the reason he was drawn to her. Not the fact that he found her attractive.

"He sure is a good-looking horse." Alex ran a hand over the gelding's withers, then down his shoulder, admiring the chestnut's well-defined muscle.

"Thanks." Caitlin smiled at Hallie. "I'll tell you what. Let's walk him up to the paddock to get reacquainted with Silver Fox. That way he'll calm down more quickly. We'll tie him to the fence and you can brush him there. How's that sound?"

"Great. Let's go."

Alex followed along.

"Hey, Cate, I'm going to take off," Dillon called. "Unless you need me here."

"Nope." She waved over her shoulder. "Thanks for doing me this favor."

"You're welcome. See you later." He nodded at Alex again, before driving away.

At the paddock, Red Fire sniffed noses with Silver Fox over the fence. The two geldings snuffled and snorted in greeting, nostrils wide, necks arched, then settled down like the old friends they were. Caitlin laughed. "You missed each other, didn't you?" She tied the lead rope to a fence post then motioned for Hallie. "Come on. We'll get the things you need to groom him."

Alex watched them go, wondering how long Caitlin would need the cane that hindered her progress.

Too bad he couldn't have met Caitlin at a different time in their lives.

ALEX SAT at his desk on Monday, trying to focus on the video game he'd started working on last week. He needed more coffee. Maybe a jolt of caffeine would take his mind off Caitlin. In the kitchen, he filled his favorite oversize mug and was about to head back to the computer when he noticed a wad of paper on the floor between the trash can and the cupboards. He bent to retrieve it, intending to throw it away, then curious, unfolded it instead.

It was a flyer from Hallie's school, announcing an upcoming Sadie Hawkins dance. Alex set his coffee mug on the counter before smoothing out the sheet of paper beside it. Why hadn't Hallie shown it to him? She hadn't even mentioned the dance. As he read the flyer in detail, he began to see why.

The dance was being done a bit differently than the typical Sadie Hawkins tradition. It was set up to be a family event. The students were supposed to bring both a date and a parent or other relative. In turn, that parent or relative was to invite a date as well. The event had been dubbed "Sadie Hawkins Family Dance Night." There would be a live band and refreshments, and parents were encouraged to accept the invitation to attend. Volunteers were also needed to act as chaperones.

Alex's heart leaped as Caitlin's name came immediately to mind. Would she want to go with him? *Never mind.* His first concern was Hallie. It worried him that she'd thrown the flyer in the trash—even if her aim was off. Just another example of how she'd changed since Melissa's death. She used to love school events. Making a mental note to have a talk with Hallie when she got home, Alex tucked the flyer under the napkin holder on the kitchen table, then went back to his computer and forced himself to work.

At four o'clock he heard the school bus pull up outside. Turning off the computer, he went to the kitchen to wait for Hallie. When she didn't come in, he looked through the window and saw her at Caitlin's paddock, petting Red Fire and Fox, offering them grass. He shook his head and laughed, not surprised. For a moment he held his breath, wondering if Caitlin would also see Hallie and come outside. But she didn't, and a short time later, Hallie headed back across the road to the house.

Alex ducked away from the window and began to prepare a snack as an excuse to linger in the kitchen. He looked up from the platter of baby carrot sticks, sliced celery and ranch dip as Hallie came through the door.

"Hi, honey. How was your day?"

She let her backpack slide off her shoulder onto the table. "Same as always. It was there."

"That good, huh?" She only looked at him, then at the plate of vegetables.

"I love ranch dip." She dragged a baby carrot through the dip and stuffed it into her mouth, quickly following it with another.

"Slow down, you'll choke." He moved toward the refrigerator. "What do you want to drink? Juice? Milk?"

"Pepsi."

"That doesn't go well with vegetables."

"It does to me."

"Okay." He shook his head. "Half health food, half junk. You must take after your old man." Then he sobered as Hallie grabbed a Pepsi and started to head for her room, her backpack hooked over one arm.

"Hal, hang on a second."

She turned to look at him expectantly. "What?"

"I want to talk to you about something." He carried the platter of veggies to the table and pulled out a chair. "Come sit down a minute."

She slumped into the chair. "I've got homework."

"That's fine. This won't take long." He pulled the crumpled Sadie Hawkins flyer out from beneath the napkin holder. "Why didn't you show this to me?"

Hallie's eyes darkened. "I threw that away."

"You missed," he said quietly. "It was on the floor."

She scooped another carrot into the ranch dressing. "It's no biggie. Just a dumb dance. I don't want to go, so I threw the flyer away."

"Honey, you always show me everything you bring home from school." Or at least she used to. "Why not this?"

"God, Dad, are you dense?"

He narrowed his eyes and she immediately dropped her gaze to her lap. "Sorry. But you don't get it."

"Get what? That you don't like doing fun things at school anymore without Melissa?" He covered her hand with his. "Hal, remember what we talked about with your counselor? You need to do fun things. Keeping busy keeps your mind busy. Life isn't always fair, but we have to keep going as best we can."

She pulled her hand away and stuffed another carrot into her mouth, speaking around it as she crunched. "It's not that."

"Don't talk with your mouth full." He waited until she swallowed. "What is it, then?"

"Duh, Dad." She gestured with both hands. "Look at the flyer. You're supposed to bring a parent and their date. Which means everyone will be inviting their mom and dad."

Crap. He was *dense.*

"Honey, not everyone has a mom and dad. A lot of kids' parents are divorced."

"Yeah. And that means they still have two parents. A stepmom, or a mother and her boyfriend or something. I don't know any boys well enough to ask them out, and even if I did, you don't have a girlfriend."

This time her name blurted from his lips. "What if I ask Caitlin?"

Hallie leaned back in her chair. "Do you think she'd come?" Her brow crinkled in a frown. "She's pretty self-conscious about her cane and her limp and all that."

"And you're pretty darned perceptive." He leaned forward and took a scoop of the dip himself, pausing with a celery stick partway to his mouth. "You know, this dance might be good for Caitlin. Maybe she needs to get out, too. Heck, so do I for that matter. So, if I ask her, will you find a boy to invite?" He gave her a conspiratorial grin, and his heart soared as she finally returned his smile.

"I guess I can come up with someone." She rose from her chair, grabbing up a handful of carrots and celery to take with her to her room. "But only if you ask Caitlin first. That way you can't chicken out."

He threw a carrot at her and she ducked, laughing.

CAITLIN SAT in the living room with the television on, not really paying attention to the early newscast. Her thoughts kept drifting back to the previous evening when Shauna had come over for their movie night.

It felt good to be with her friend again, doing something familiar and fun, laughing and talking about their two favorite subjects—horses and men.

"How come you didn't tell me your neighbor is such a hottie?" Shauna had asked. "I saw him out in his yard when I pulled in." She'd waved her hand in front of her face. "Whew!"

Caitlin had only smirked. "He's hot all right, not that it matters."

Her comment had evoked a tongue-lashing from Shauna. "You're as gorgeous as ever, not to mention a good person."

Right.

Caitlin glared at her cane, propped against the nearby ottoman. How much longer would she have to use it? She hated being a whiner. But it was hard to get rid of the resentment she'd carried ever since the crash. She hated Lester Godfrey—the drunk who'd slammed his SUV into her Jag—and was glad he'd been arrested. She hoped he spent the rest of his life in prison.

A knock interrupted her thoughts. Spike raced to the door, barking. Expecting Hallie, Caitlin called out, "Come in."

Alex opened the door and stepped inside. "Hi. What are you doing all shut up in here? It's still pretty warm outside."

Hiding. She choked back the reply and forced a smile. "Just watching the news."

"That sounds depressing." He stood near the sofa, and pulled something from his jeans pocket. "May I?" He indicated the empty seat beside her, and Caitlin nodded.

"Of course. What have you got there?"

He handed her the paper as Spike jumped into his lap. "A flyer from Hallie's school." He gave her a moment to read it, then asked, "Would you like to go?"

"To the dance?" She stared at him.

"No, to the moon." His crooked grin gave her butterflies in her stomach.

She looked at him as if he'd taken leave of his senses. "Yeah, sure. Maybe I can do a tap-dance routine with my cane."

He sobered. "Caitlin, don't be so hard on yourself. Come on, it'll be fun. You can manage a slow one. I'll let you lean on me."

Her heart skipped a beat. *Lordy.* She'd love to have a man like him to lean on. If things were different.

"I don't think so."

"Why not?"

She stared at him, exasperated. "You sound like Shauna—my best friend. Isn't it obvious?" She gestured at her body. "I'm in no shape to dance."

"I thought you were made of tougher stuff than that."

"What's that supposed to mean?"

"Just what I said. From what I've heard and seen, you've come a long way since your accident."

"Yeah, well, I've got a lot further to go. And I don't think a school dance is going to help."

"Would you do it for Hallie?"

She scowled at him. "Using your daughter to get a date is not cool, Alex."

"I'm not using her. I'm asking you to help *her*." The sorrow in his eyes was enough to undo Caitlin. "She's had a pretty tough time of it since Melissa's death. She doesn't take much interest in anything these days. So you can imagine how happy I am that she wants to ride Red Fire and hang out here with you and your dog." He ruffled Spike's ears.

"I'm glad to hear that. I like Hallie a lot. But I'm still not following you." Caitlin paused. "What does this have to do with her?"

"She won't go unless I bring someone. The other kids will have two parents."

She felt her face flush at the idea of filling the role of Hallie's other parent. She was definitely not mother material. "I see."

"So will you go?"

"Don't you have a girlfriend?" Her face grew even hotter. If he did, it was none of her business.

He laughed. "Between work and Hallie, that's all I have time for."

Relief mingled with her disappointment. "Okay. So this wouldn't be an actual date then."

"No." He lowered his eyes as though taking great interest in scratching Spike under the chin. "Just an outing between friends. It'll be fun."

"Do I have to dress the part?"

"I didn't think about that, but since it is a Sadie Hawkins dance, I'll bet some form of hillbilly-like attire will work."

"I don't have anything to wear that would fall into that category."

"Neither does Hallie. Guess we'll have to go shopping. You're welcome to join us."

"Thanks." She shrugged. "We were going to look at saddles in town anyway. The feed store carries bib overalls and flannel shirts."

"All right, then. When do you want to go?"

She looked at the flyer. "The dance is a week from Saturday, so that gives us plenty of time. But I'm betting Hallie is eager to get her saddle."

"She is. I've got a ton of work to do this week, but I can make some time on whatever day is good for you."

"I'm pretty open. My therapy sessions are usually in the mornings, so we can go any day after Hallie gets home from school if that suits you. Just give me a call."

"Okay." He gave Spike a final pat, then stood.

"See you later." He paused with his hand on the door-knob. "Are you sure you don't need some help with your chores?"

She hated to admit that she did. She'd managed to feed the horses the past few days, but Hallie had been a big help. "You can send Hallie over if she wants to come, but it's not necessary. I mean, she's welcome to hang around the horses, but she doesn't have to help with the chores."

"She thinks caring for the horses is fun. She doesn't look at it as work. Besides, if she wants to own a horse, she needs to realize it's a lot of respon-sibility." He grinned that damned, sexy, crooked grin of his, making her stomach tighten.

"All right," Caitlin said. "I feed the horses at five, if that doesn't interfere with your dinner."

"Not at all." He opened the door, then lifted his hand in a wave. "Later."

"You can leave that open," Caitlin said.

She watched him walk out onto the porch, admir-ing the strong line of his physique. His well-formed physique. The way the late afternoon sun played on his dark hair....

She loved how he looked in his cowboy hat, but she loved him without it, too. He had thick, wavy hair. Hair she wouldn't mind running her hands through.

Just an outing between friends.

Right.

She stroked Spike's fur, remembering Alex's long, tanned fingers, scratching the dog's ears. Being "just friends" with Alex was like owning a Maserati without driving it.

Caitlin sat there, feeling like a teenager who'd lost her license.

CHAPTER SEVEN

CAITLIN LEANED against the paddock rail, watching Hallie and Red Fire. Out of the corner of her eye she also watched Alex as he observed his daughter's newfound riding skills with pride and nervousness. "Relax," she said. "She'll be fine."

He winced. "I know. But a horse is a big animal."

"Yeah, and the world's a big place. It'll be okay, Alex."

Hallie nudged Red Fire into a trot, bringing him over to stand in front of them. The leather of the secondhand saddle Alex had purchased three days ago creaked as she shifted. "I'm bored." She looked at Caitlin, then her dad. "When can I start riding on the trails? Or down the road or something?" She gestured toward the dirt-and-gravel road. "There's plenty of room on the shoulder."

"I don't think so," Alex said. "A car could come by and spook your horse. Until you've had a little more experience, I'm afraid you're stuck in the paddock, Hal. Or in the arena at the house once I get it repaired."

"Da-ad." Hallie slumped in the saddle. "Red Fire won't spook. Will he, Caitlin?"

"It's not likely, but you're not ready to go down the road just yet. You need some lessons first."

"But I'm sick of riding in a circle."

"Hey." Alex laid his hand on Red Fire's muzzle, stroking the gelding's jaw with the other hand. "I thought you were happy to have a horse to ride at all."

"I am," Hallie said. She wrinkled her nose. "Sorry, Caitlin. I didn't mean to be rude."

Caitlin smiled. "I understand."

"What would you say to a compromise?" Alex asked.

It took Caitlin a moment to realize he was asking her as well as Hallie.

"What do you mean?" Hallie asked.

"You could ride in the field." Alex indicated the pasture behind the house. "That way you'd still be in an enclosed area with no traffic to worry about."

"I don't think that's such a good idea," Caitlin interrupted.

He raised his eyebrows. "Now who's being the worrywart?"

She stared at him. "I can't believe you said that."

"Come on, Caitlin," Hallie begged. "Even Dad thinks it's okay."

She gave a dry laugh. "Your dad is forgetting that even the most gentle of horses *can* spook. Alex, there's barbed wire out there. Dillon doesn't have the hot wire completely run around the perimeter yet."

She spoke to Hallie once more. "You'll be riding in the pasture and on the trails before you know it, kiddo. Your dad will line up someone to give you lessons, I'm sure." She gave Alex a meaningful look.

Hallie's face fell. "I thought you were giving me lessons."

Caitlin took a deep breath. "I'm not able to ride yet, Hallie. Remember?"

"Oh."

Caitlin paused. "You know what? You're not ready to go it alone, but I think you'd be okay for a little ride in the pasture if your dad goes with you. We can saddle up Silver Fox for him."

"No way." Alex shook his head. "Red Fire's one thing. But I'm not getting on that ten-foot-tall monster, riding a saddle the size of a postage stamp."

Caitlin hid a smile. "That rusty, huh, cowboy? I suppose you're right, then. He's a lot of horse."

"Exactly."

"Dad, don't be such a wuss," Hallie said. "Ride with me."

"No. I'm not going to see you hurt because I'm not up to speed on my horsemanship. Now do you want to ride in the paddock, or would you rather un-saddle Red Fire and call it a day?"

Hallie sighed. "Fine." She turned the gelding around and went back to trotting around the enclo-sure.

"I can give you the names of some good riding in-structors," Caitlin said.

"You're afraid."

She'd been focused on Hallie. Now she turned to look squarely at him. "What?"

"You heard me. I know you can't jump anymore. But I don't understand what's stopping you from getting back on your horse."

Her jaw dropped. "Who the hell do you think you are, passing judgment on me? I told you...I *can't* ride."

"Not can't. Won't."

She fought the urge to bop him upside the head with her cane. "You've known me how long?"

"Long enough to see what a fighter you are. You're walking better than you were last week. I'm betting you won't be needing that cane much longer. And you've been feeding your horses."

"With Hallie's help."

"Yeah, in the evenings. But I doubt those horses only eat once a day. Right?"

"Your point being?"

"Anyone who's strong-willed enough to do things for herself, to move out on her own when most people would take full advantage of the staff and family you have to care for you…" He ticked the list off on his fingers. "Who would drive her truck when she's not supposed to and push herself so hard she's plain exhausted most of the time, is tough enough to get on a horse and ride him at a slow walk."

She continued to stare at him. "Silver Fox is a lot of horse."

He took a step closer, glancing over to make sure Hallie was out of earshot, then lowered his voice. "And you're a lot of woman."

For one split, crazy second Caitlin thought he was going to kiss her. And for two crazy seconds, she knew she would let him.

Except that he didn't. "Caitlin, if things were different in my life…well, let's just say you're a good-looking woman. You're tough and a go-getter, and I damned well know the only thing stopping you from riding is fear."

"You're full of it."

"I don't think so." He gave her a cocky look. "Riding is your life. And you don't want to chance failing."

She took a step back, unconsciously close to letting go of her cane. She wasn't sure what made her mad the most—his crassness or her desire to kiss him. It was only Hallie's presence that kept her from giving Alex a piece of her mind.

Caitlin trembled.

"Prove me wrong. Saddle up your horse and ride with Hallie."

"This isn't high school, cowboy. I don't have to prove a thing to you." She turned away, her eyes locked on Hallie.

Alex took her by the arm, his touch firm but gentle. "I'm not playing games, Caitlin, and I'm not asking you to prove anything to me." His dark eyes held hers. "Prove it to yourself." He nodded toward Silver Fox, who walked along behind Hallie and Red Fire. "Get back on the horse."

"I wasn't bucked off."

"In a sense you were."

"I was hit by a drunk, Alex." She jerked her arm from his grasp. "A drunken, stupid fool who ruined my life!" Hot tears clogged her throat, and stung the back of her eyes. "I was a grand prix rider. Now I can barely walk." With effort, she lowered her voice as Hallie looked their way. Caitlin turned her back to the paddock and leaned against the fence, folding her arms. "So don't tell me I'm scared. You don't have a clue."

Alex's expression softened, his face flushed. "I'm sorry, Caitlin." He moved as though to touch her, then let his hand fall at his side. "I was only trying to help."

"Yeah, well thanks for the armchair psychiatry. I

can handle my own business." She took a deep breath, then turned back, forcing a smile for Hallie. She had no intention of ruining the kid's fun just because her dad was being a jackass.

"You're looking good there, kiddo. Best circles I've ever seen. We'll figure out a way for you to have more fun next time."

"Speaking of next time," Alex said, "let's call it a day, Hallie. You've got homework."

"All right." Hallie rode over to the fence and dismounted. "Thanks, Caitlin."

"You're more than welcome." Caitlin walked beside her as Hallie led the horse toward the barn. "I've got the phone numbers for a couple of people who give riding lessons. I'll get them for your dad, and we'll work on springing you out of the paddock."

Hallie's expression darkened. "I don't want anyone else to teach me. I want you."

At a loss for words, Caitlin silently pleaded for Alex to help her out of this corner she'd pinned herself in. He said nothing.

"I'd love to be able to do that. But I already told you, I can't. You need someone who can actually demonstrate techniques."

Hallie shrugged. "I'm doing okay with the way we've been going. You can just tell me what to do and I'll do it."

This time Caitlin looked straight at Alex. But he pretended grave interest in studying the evening sky.

"All right," she said, vowing to choke him. "We'll try it for a while longer. But if I still think you need proper lessons, will you let me put you in touch with someone good?"

"You are someone good," Hallie said.

IF IT WEREN'T for Hallie, Alex would've changed his mind about going to the Sadie Hawkins dance. True, she hadn't wanted to go at first, but after their shopping trip with Caitlin this past Wednesday for the saddle, and the clothes they planned to wear to the dance, Hallie had quickly gotten into the spirit of things. He'd already known she looked up to Caitlin. But the more Hallie was around her, the more she seemed drawn to the woman.

He hoped he hadn't made a mistake letting his daughter get close to her. Hallie already felt abandoned by her mother... He didn't want her getting too attached and getting hurt again. For that matter, he didn't plan to risk his own heart anytime soon.

"Dad, are you ready yet?" Hallie paused in the doorway of his room where Alex stood holding the straw hat he'd bought as part of his costume.

Like him, she wore bib overalls and a flannel shirt. Her hair was in braids and she'd drawn freckles on her cheeks with a makeup pencil. They'd go. They'd have fun. End of story. He'd worry about the rest later.

"Yep, as ready as I can be." He put the hat on and tweaked the brim of Hallie's. "Let's go get Caitlin."

She was already waiting, sitting on the front porch, when he pulled up. She looked mighty cute. The feed store hadn't had any overalls that fit her, and she'd told him she'd figure something else out. And she had.

The blue denim skirt she wore with a red-and-white polka-dot, off-the-shoulder blouse hit her mid-thigh, showing off her legs. She'd put on hiking boots in an effort to look corny and wore her hair in pigtails. But even the clunky hiking boots couldn't take away from the fact that she was one good-looking woman. Especially in pigtails.

"You look great. Really authentic."

"You, too." She climbed into the truck with only a little awkwardness.

Her left leg seemed a bit stiff, and he wondered if she was in pain.

"I'm afraid this cane doesn't do much to add to my costume, though." Caitlin grimaced.

"Actually, it's sort of cool," Hallie said. She grinned. "You can pretend to be the old granny from the mountains."

"Old granny, huh?" Caitlin frowned. "Thanks a lot, kiddo."

"You're welcome." Hallie giggled, and Alex knew that any hope of preventing his daughter from getting closer to Caitlin was a lost cause.

The school parking lot was already crowded when they pulled in. "Want me to let you girls off up front while I park?"

"I'm fine." She looked at him as though reading his mind. "You can park wherever and we'll walk."

"Okay." Once he'd taken care of the vehicle, he strolled back beside Caitlin while Hallie walked ahead.

"You still mad at me?" Alex asked once Hallie was out of earshot.

"I wasn't mad. Just annoyed."

"Huh." He shook his head. *Women.*

"Let's forget about it and enjoy the dance," she said. "For Hallie's sake."

"Sure. Whatever you say."

The gymnasium was decorated with crepe-paper streamers and balloons in the school colors, red and black. Straw bales lined the room along with groups of folding chairs. A concession booth, offering pop and snacks, had been set up at one end, a DJ behind a table on a makeshift stage at the other, microphone, stereo equipment and a stack of CDs at hand.

The dance soon got under way, the lighting slightly dimmed. The DJ played bluegrass and some rowdy country songs. Then he switched to soft rock and put on a slow one.

"Would you like to dance?" Alex asked, holding his hand out to Caitlin.

She hesitated, then laid her cane against a chair and took his arm. He tucked her hand through his elbow and held her tight so she wouldn't fall. He liked the way she felt snugged up against his side. It had been a good, long while since he'd held a woman.

And when he took her in his arms to sway gently to the music, he felt a rush of feelings long dormant. It wasn't only the physical attraction he felt for her. It was the pleasure of holding her protectively in his arms. Making sure she'd have no trouble dancing, wouldn't feel embarrassed in any way. Caitlin, on the other hand, seemed stiff and uncomfortable. She danced woodenly, holding her body away from his as much as she could without making it too obvious.

"Relax," he said, tugging her closer. "Lean on me." He wrapped one arm around her waist, holding her hand lightly. Her hair smelled sweet, the subtle fragrance of flowers and herbs. He wanted to nuzzle her neck. To put both arms around her and pull her as close as he could.

He spotted Hallie with Jeremy Simms, the boy who'd ended up being her date. He lived a block away from the school, and had agreed to meet Hallie at the dance rather than have them pick him up. The two of them danced together, somewhat awkwardly, but they were talking, and Hallie seemed to be having a good time. It warmed Alex's heart.

He turned his attention back to Caitlin, smiling as he looked down into her eyes. She was nearly a foot shorter than him, and she felt like a fragile doll in his arms. But he knew that was an illusion. "See, this isn't so bad."

"It beats going to the dentist," she said, then laughed as his smile slipped. "I'm kidding, Alex. This is very nice." She laid her head against his chest, and he groaned inwardly.

The song ended, and they went back to the folding chairs. Caitlin sank into one, looking tired, but happy.

"You okay?"

She gripped her cane, moving it out of the way. "I'm fine."

"Thirsty?"

"Sure. I could use something to drink."

"Pop or punch?"

"Do they have any juice or bottled water?"

"I'll check." He turned to leave just as Hallie hurried over.

"Dad, can I get something from the snack booth?"

"You bet. Come on, I'm headed that way." He started to slip his arm around her shoulders, but realized that might embarrass her. "Where's your date?"

She blushed. "Jeremy's not a date, Dad. Just a friend."

"Fine. Sorry."

"He's talking to his buddies. I'm okay with that."

He grinned. "A woman of independence. I like that." At the snack booth, he waited in line with her. Hallie chose a soft drink and nacho chips drenched in cheese and jalapeños.

"Can I have a chocolate bar, too?"

"Good grief." He pulled out his wallet. "You're going to get sick if you eat all that junk."

"No, I won't." She leaned against the counter. "I'm hungry."

"Okay." He laughed and bought her what she wanted. She gathered up her goodies, thanked him and took off again.

Back at the folding chairs, he handed Caitlin a bottle of some kind of sports drink. "That was the closest thing to juice they had."

"Thank you." She unscrewed the lid and took a sip.

"Are you hungry? I didn't think to ask."

She shook her head. "I ate something before I left the house."

"So did we, but you'd never know it to watch Hallie." He chuckled. "I don't know where she puts everything she eats. You should've seen what she made me buy."

"She does seem to like junk," Caitlin said. Then she winced. "Sorry. I'm being nosy, aren't I?"

"I take it you have an aversion to junk food?"

"I've always tried to keep my body in good shape for riding." Her smile faded as she looked down at her cane.

Self-consciously, she tugged at the hem of her skirt and, for the first time, Alex noticed a scar on the inside of one knee.

"I guess that's a good thing," he said.

"Yeah, but it doesn't much matter now." She shrugged. "I can't jump, and I…"

"What?"

Her face reddened. "Nothing."

"No, what were you going to say?"

She gave a half smile. "I used to care about my weight and my figure."

"And?"

"Let's just say I don't exactly feel sexy anymore."

"I don't think you have any worries there." He cleared his throat. "There's not a single thing wrong with the way you look, Caitlin."

She turned away from him, sipping her drink. "Is Hallie having a good time?"

He followed her line of sight to where Hallie sat in the far corner with a friend. Both girls were chowing down on chips, candy and soft drinks.

"Seems to be. But she got after me for calling Jeremy her date."

Caitlin grinned. "Twelve's an awkward age. Not a little girl, not yet a woman."

"Yeah." He sipped his Pepsi. "Sometimes I wish her mother was around to help her out with stuff."

"Where is her mom? If you don't mind my asking."

He did mind, and was sorry he'd mentioned Julie. "She's out of the picture. She left when Hallie was small."

"She doesn't visit her?"

"Can we talk about something else?"

"Sure. Sorry." She turned away, and without thinking, he laid his hand on her knee.

"No, I'm the one who's sorry, Caitlin. I brought it up."

"It's okay. I shouldn't have pried." She shifted uncomfortably, and he moved his hand. "Hallie's a good kid."

"Yes, she is."

"I've been thinking about what you said last night."

He grunted. "Which part?"

"About me being scared to ride."

"I shouldn't have said that. I told you I didn't mean it."

"It's okay. You're right, you know. I am scared." Her blue eyes grew serious. "I know I'll never get back to the way I was, and I don't like that. It makes me feel...helpless."

"Far from it. And if you want to ride again, then do it." Before she could protest, he rushed on. "Sure, maybe you'll never be able to jump again. But then, maybe you will."

"I don't think so." She laughed dryly. "My head injuries were pretty severe. I couldn't even sit up or feed myself when I came out of the coma."

He'd read she'd been in the coma for nine days. "That must've been tough."

"It was." She paused again. "I suppose I've always been the sort of person who never does anything halfway. For me, it's all or nothing."

"So, since you can't jump it's nothing? You choose not to ever ride a horse again?"

She stared at him. "Boy, when you put it that way, it sounds really bad. I can't imagine never riding...."

"Hey, it's your decision," he said. He didn't want to make her feel bad. "There's more to life than riding horses."

"Not for me there isn't."

CAITLIN WISHED the evening was over. Her legs were beginning to ache, and her back throbbed. She'd danced to a few slow songs with Alex, and tried one fast one when he and Hallie prodded her. But the effort had proven too much. She'd made a joke of it, said she'd better sit down before she fell down. But that hadn't been so far from the truth. She sat watching Alex dance a fast country swing with the school principal, a woman who had to be seventy if she was a day. But you'd never know it from the way she danced. Alex was actually having a hard time keeping up with Mrs. Zane.

In need of a bathroom break, Caitlin made her way from the gym, down the hall to the girls' restroom. As she opened the door, she heard the sound of someone being sick inside one of the stalls. *Poor kid.* She hesitated, wondering if she should leave and not embarrass the girl. But then she spotted a familiar pair of boots beneath the metal dividing wall. A moment later the stall door opened, and Hallie stepped out.

"Hallie." Caitlin touched her shoulder. "Are you all right?"

Hallie's eyes widened, then she lowered them and nodded as she hurried to the sink. "I'm okay."

Caitlin stayed where she was, still worried. "Too much junk food?" She recalled seeing Hallie pay more than one visit to the snack booth.

"Yeah." Hallie nodded, not meeting her gaze in the mirror. She leaned over the sink, rinsed her mouth out and washed her face, then reached for a paper towel. Sweat beaded her forehead beneath the brim of her straw hat.

Caitlin frowned. "Are you sure you're all right?"

"I'm fine. Like you said, just too much junk."

"Okay." She paused. "Are you having a good time?"

Hallie wrinkled her nose. "I guess so."

"Jeremy's pretty hot." Caitlin gave her a conspiratorial smile, hoping to get one in return. She hated to see Hallie's fun ruined by her father's overindulgence.

"He's okay."

Caitlin nodded. "Well, I guess I'll see you back in the gym." She headed for a stall while Hallie scurried away.

CHAPTER EIGHT

A WEEK AFTER the dance the weather turned cool and crisp with the coming of October. The leaves began to wilt off the trees like tired runners nearing the end of a marathon. Caitlin stood in the backyard. In the distance, she saw Red Fire and Silver Fox grazing in the midday rays of the sun. Dillon had finished the electric fencing a few days ago, and the two geldings seemed to be enjoying the freedom of running on pasture.

Caitlin loved this time of year. Some of her best childhood memories were of trail riding with Dillon, their horses' hooves crunching on the autumn leaves. Hallie seemed to be enjoying the fall weather, too. She came over at least three afternoons a week to ride—and pretty much every day to help feed. Watching her with Red Fire made Caitlin want badly to ride.

Maybe she was scared to try. And maybe she shouldn't be. She was relying less on her cane.... And she was coping with the dizzy spells.

As she watched the sun playing on Red Fire's bright coat, she knew Alex was right. She might not be able to jump anymore, but that didn't mean she couldn't get on a horse. Besides, she trusted Red Fire. Hallie's school bus wouldn't arrive for another two hours. That gave her plenty of time to take the gelding for a short ride.

Caitlin laughed. It wasn't as though she would tire the horse. She looked toward Alex's house. She didn't want him to see what she was doing. Somehow, it was important to her to do this alone, with no one watching. His truck wasn't even in the driveway. Good.

Leaving Spike in the backyard, Caitlin walked to the barn. Inside, the familiar odors of hay and wood shavings suddenly brought back memories of the last time she'd ridden. The ride she and Shauna had planned to take before Caitlin returned to school. The way the snow had fallen that night as she left Shauna's house.

Big, heavy flakes.

Black, wet pavement and the exploding sound of metal on metal.

She shook her head, forcing everything from her mind except the task at hand. From the tack room, she took her saddle—the one Hallie had been using prior to getting her own. Caitlin hadn't brought any of her riding attire with her when she'd moved. She'd have to ride in her jeans and tennis shoes. Not the safest footwear, but her adrenaline was pumping too fast to turn back now.

As she lifted the saddle, the weight and feel of it meant something entirely different than it had when she'd saddled the horse for Hallie. Familiar excitement surged through her in anticipation of the ride. Exhilaration, freedom. Being on a horse was like sailing on the wind, leaving your cares behind you, while you floated above the ground.

Caitlin laid the saddle in the aisle with an assortment of tack and grooming tools, then went outside to call Red Fire. Again, she glanced over to make sure Alex's truck wasn't there. She hoped he stayed wherever he was. Red Fire and Silver Fox both came readily, knowing she had something for them. They lipped the apple-flavored treats from her palm, then nudged her, looking for more.

"That's it," she said, laughing. She cupped Red Fire's head in her hands and rubbed her face against his muzzle. "It's just you and me, boy. Like old times." She slipped a nylon halter on him and led him into the barn.

In the aisle, she put him in cross ties, her hands cold with nervous anticipation as she brushed him, then tacked him up. "You can do this," she chided herself. "And it took a rusty cowboy to remind you."

Rusty, but good-looking.

Caitlin led Red Fire into the paddock, where she

adjusted her stirrups. Maybe she ought to take a trial run in the smaller enclosure first, before proceeding to the pasture. Her spirits sank as she raised her left foot to the stirrup. She couldn't flex her knee, and her leg wouldn't rise high enough to slide her foot into the stirrup.

"That's okay," she said to herself and the horse. "We can mount on the right." It was an old wives' tale that a horse would spook if you mounted from its right side. Any well-trained horse should let its rider up on either side. Caitlin gathered her reins once more and put her right foot in the stirrup. But her sense of accomplishment was short-lived as she hoisted her left leg up. Her muscles were too weak to swing high enough. She hung there, halfway in the saddle. Clumsy. Dizzy. To his credit, Red Fire stood stock-still.

With a gasp, she sank to the ground, nearly losing her balance as she tried to untangle her foot from the stirrup. Sweat beaded her upper lip and forehead.

She stood, weak and shaky, angry at her own body. "Damn it!" She wasn't giving up that easy. "Come on, boy." She took hold of the reins looped around Red Fire's neck and led him over to the fence. Carefully, she lined him up parallel to the wooden rails, then pulled herself up onto them. It took every ounce of her strength to do it, but once she was there, she was able to swing onto Red Fire's back. Her legs and arms felt like limp noodles, but she got both feet into the stirrups, and felt exhilarated.

"We did it." She patted Red Fire's neck, then eased him into a walk. *God, but it felt heavenly to be back on her horse.* She glanced over at Alex's empty house and mouthed a silent thank-you to him for prodding her. As she circled the paddock, she began to relax. Her left hip ached, and her foot felt awkward in the stirrup, but by God she was riding. She would've loved to try posting a trot, but decided against it. For now, she'd have to be content with a slow walk. Feeling like a beginner, Caitlin circled the paddock a half-dozen times, then paused at the gate.

Red Fire was trained well enough to let her open it from his back. But could she balance well enough to do it? If she got down, she might not have the strength to climb back up, and that was a risk she wasn't willing to take. She itched to be out riding in the pasture. Cuing Red Fire into a side pass, Caitlin leaned carefully from the saddle to unlatch the gate. It took her two tries, but she got it. She swung it open triumphantly. At least she didn't need to worry about shutting it again, since there were no horses in the paddock. From the pasture, Silver Fox whickered and walked toward her to see what was going on.

"Hey, pretty boy." She leaned over and patted his shoulder as he stepped alongside Red Fire. If only she could ride him. Sail over fences, crouching low on his neck as though the two of them were one.

But that wasn't happening.

Guiding Red Fire away from Fox, Caitlin headed across the pasture. The gray gelding tagged along for a while, then lost interest and resumed grazing. Caitlin rode straight down the middle of the acreage, then turned to follow the fence line once she got close to the dirt road. She kept enough distance between her horse and the hot wire to be safe. Following the fence would give her a longer ride than just criss-crossing the pasture, or riding in figure eights. She longed to head out on the trail, and thought of Hallie. She couldn't blame the kid for being bored with going in circles.

Alex really ought to get a horse for himself. That way he could ride with his daughter. And maybe, just maybe, the day would come when Caitlin could regain her balance and composure well enough to take Silver Fox out on the trail with them. The idea of turning her grand prix jumper into an ordinary trail horse left a bitter taste in her mouth. Fox deserved more than that.

Caitlin was so lost in thought, it took her a minute to notice the dog trotting along the shoulder of the road. Big and black, he looked like a Labrador mix of some sort. His tongue lolled between his teeth as he turned to duck under the barbed wire fence, heading straight at Red Fire.

Caitlin tensed in the saddle. Not in fear of the dog, but because she knew what Red Fire would do. The gelding hated big dogs, and had been known to charge whenever one came near him. He'd once chased a trio of strays out of the pasture at Foxwood Farms, striking and stomping at them with his front hooves.

"Easy, boy," she said. The gelding raised his head as the Lab sped toward them. "Go home, fella," Caitlin called. "Go on, get!" But the dog paid her no mind. Instead, he trotted closer to Red Fire. He didn't growl, but he didn't wag his tail, either. She couldn't tell what his intentions were. Dogs that chased horses normally posed more of a danger to the horse than themselves. A horse could be severely injured being run through a fence. Or bitten.

But in this case, Caitlin knew Red Fire would be the one doing the chasing, and she wasn't sure she could hold him back. Normally, he would never misbehave while under saddle. But when he saw a big dog, he seemed to get tunnel vision, and it took all her strength and skill to hold him back. Skill and strength she wasn't so sure she had anymore.

"Go on!" Caitlin commanded the dog. "Easy, Red Fire. It's okay."

The gelding pinned his ears and snaked his neck out as far as he could under Caitlin's firm hand. He began to move in circles as the Lab worked its way around him, now mere feet away. Caitlin took a firmer hold of the leather reins and nudged the horse into a walk, hoping to distract him and move past the dog. Hoping the dog would also lose interest and go on his way. Instead, the Lab moved in and sniffed Red Fire's back leg. The horse spun to face him, ears flattened. Caitlin was dizzy. "Easy, easy," she repeated. She focused both on balancing in the saddle and trying her best to separate horse and dog. Maybe she should try to dismount. But what if the dog attacked?

As if on cue, the Lab dived at Red Fire's heels. The horse kicked out, then spun again to dive at the Lab, striking out with his front hooves. The dog tucked his tail, but instead of running, he became agitated. He barked with fervor, and lunged once more toward the horse. Abandoning all thought of speaking calmly so as not to upset her horse, Caitlin shouted at the top of her lungs. "Go on! Get out of here, damn you!" She let go of the reins with one hand and waved her arm at the dog, to no avail.

He flat-out attacked her horse, letting out a volley of barks and growls as he attempted to bite Red Fire in the flanks. The gelding kicked at him hard, and Caitlin nearly lost her seat. Gasping, she grabbed a handful of mane, clinging desperately with one hand, while attempting to control the reins with the other. Her weak knees clamped the saddle, but her left one had gone numb, and she wasn't sure she could hang on much longer. Red Fire spun yet again, this time diving at the dog with a vengeance.

In desperation, she dropped the reins, giving Red Fire his head, and leaned forward in the saddle. The shift in her body weight let the horse know he was free to move forward, and he did without hesitation. He jumped and struck at the dog, clipping the animal with at least one front hoof. The Lab let out a startled yip and darted away, then ignorantly came back for more.

Red Fire circled to strike out at him again, and the ground whirled around Caitlin with a merry-go-round effect. She wanted to close her eyes, but knew that would make it worse. She was going to fall. There was no way she could stay in the saddle a moment longer. Everything around her blurred, and she kicked free of the stirrups, worried about getting hung up on her way down. Terrified of being dragged to death by an enraged horse who was focused only on the dog that tormented him.

Somewhere in the back of her mind, she heard a shout. Had she yelled at the dog again? She felt sick, and dizzy, and foolish. Then she was tumbling from the saddle.

And then Caitlin realized she wasn't falling at all. Strong arms encircled her waist. She'd been yanked from the saddle. By Alex. He'd been the one shouting at the dog. And now he held her against him after having scooped her from the back of her horse. He cradled her in his arms like a groom carrying his bride. Only grooms didn't usually shout this way, Caitlin thought deliriously.

Like the night of the crash, everything seemed to be in slow motion.

Alex, holding her, shouting at the dog.

Red Fire moving away.

She looked over her shoulder and saw a streak of black as the dog turned tail and ran. She caught a glimpse of the chestnut, pounding after the dog, free of his rider.

"Don't let him hit the fence!" Caitlin looked up into Alex's dark eyes, still dizzy. Crap, had she hit her head? She must have, because she'd wrapped her arms tightly around Alex's neck, inhaling his warm, male scent, and she had to fight against tucking her head against his chest and staying that way until her light-headedness vanished. But since Alex was causing part of her condition, she knew being in his arms was only making matters worse.

"Are you okay?" he asked.

"I'm fine," she lied. "Put me down. Catch my horse—please." Frantically, she looked once more over her shoulder, worried Red Fire would run through the fence. But he'd come to a sliding halt as the dog dived beneath the wire and took off down the road as though the hounds of hell were on his trail. *Horse from hell was more like it.*

"I'll get him in a minute," Alex said, his voice gruff, "once I make sure you're okay. What in hell were you doing?"

She wriggled in his arms, and he finally set her on her feet. She brushed the hair out of her face and tried not to sag against him. Immediately, he put his arm around her. "I'm fine," she repeated. "I just decided you were right and that I needed to get back in the saddle."

The worry in his eyes turned to regret. "Obviously, I was wrong. Caitlin, why did you try riding if you truly knew you weren't up to it? I shouldn't have pressured you. I told you the other night I was sorry."

"It's no big deal." She did her best to hide the fact that she was ready to sink to the ground. She'd never felt so wobbly in her life. "There really is no reason I shouldn't be able to take a short spin on a kid-gentle gelding. I wasn't expecting a crazy dog to chase us."

"Looked to me like your horse was the one in pursuit." The corners of his mouth twitched.

"Yeah, and that's another thing. I can't believe I didn't think about Red Fire's aversion to big dogs when I agreed to let Hallie ride him." Her heart quickened. "My God, what if that would've happened when she was on him?" She clamped a hand to her forehead. "I'm an idiot. I never gave it a thought."

"Hey, stop that." He slipped his other arm around her, holding her in a light embrace. "It didn't, and you're not. Actually, you're the one who made me see I was being overprotective. I can't watch Hallie every second of every day, even though I'd like to. And I know horseback riding comes with risks."

"So, you're not mad at me?"

In answer, he pressed a kiss to her forehead. She forgot about being dizzy. Forgot about the pain in her hip, her leg.

"Yes, I am. But not for anything that has to do with Hallie." He stared down at her, his brow furrowed. "Why didn't you wait until I was here? You could've gotten seriously hurt." He eyed her tennis shoes. "You're not even wearing boots."

"I don't have any here."

"Well maybe you should get some."

"Doesn't matter. I won't be riding again." She ignored the picture of her riding with Alex and Hallie.

"Why not?"

"What do you mean, why not? Isn't it obvious?" She gestured to her body. "I couldn't even handle a simple ride in the pasture. I'm certainly a long way from where I used to be."

He pulled her closer, and her heart raced.

"Maybe. But you've also come a long way." His eyes held hers, serious and yet what looked like tender. "Look how well you stayed on that horse. Red Fire was spinning in circles, striking out at that dog. I nearly had a heart attack when I pulled in and saw you out here. I thought for sure you were going to get thrown."

"So did I." She grimaced. "I guess I owe you for pulling me off my horse."

"Any time," he said.

Caitlin held her breath. He was going to kiss her. And not on the forehead this time.

But just then, the sound of the school bus grinding down the road reached her ears. Alex looked up, then pulled away from her as the yellow bus topped a rise in the road and came to a halt in front of the house. "There's Hallie."

"Yeah." Caitlin slipped the rest of the way from his embrace. "Good thing she didn't see the dog." She looked at her watch. "Is it four o'clock already?"

"No. School let out early. Parent-teacher conferences, which I'm going to be late for if I don't hurry up." He hesitated. "Let me help you back to the house."

She waved him away, before realizing she didn't have her cane.

He'd obviously noticed, too, because he stepped up beside her and slipped his arm around her waist.

"Come on. Let me walk you back, then I'll get your horse. He's fine." He glanced back at the gelding. "He's just grazing."

"I don't want him to step on his reins and get tangled," Caitlin said, standing her ground. "Would you catch him, please?"

"Sure, all right. Here comes Hallie anyway."

She'd ducked through the fence when she'd spotted them. Now she broke into a run. "Caitlin! What's going on?" She knit her brows together. "I saw Red Fire running loose with his saddle on, and you and Dad… Were you riding? Did you fall?"

"Yes and no," Caitlin said, forcing a chuckle. "Red Fire and I had a little run-in with a dog. Walk me back to the barn and I'll explain." She reached out and slipped her arm around Hallie's shoulders, glad for an excuse not to hang on to Alex anymore. He'd already turned away to catch Red Fire. "Mind if I lean on you, kiddo? I left my cane back in the paddock."

"Sure. So, what happened?"

Caitlin explained, and Hallie looked up at her, eyes wide. "Wow! That took some guts." She grinned. "So, you wanna get back on?"

"What?" Caitlin laughed.

"You know. They always say when you fall off, you need to get back on the horse."

"But I didn't fall."

"Not technically."

Caitlin rolled her tongue against her cheek. "Yeah, I guess I would have if your dad hadn't rescued me."

Hallie grinned. "He's a real hero, huh?"

"I heard that," Alex said, coming up behind them leading Red Fire. "And I highly resemble that remark."

Hallie groaned, and Caitlin shook her head, laughing, trying not to think about the way it had felt to be in Alex's arms. To have his lips touch her. She shivered involuntarily.

"Are you cold?" Hallie frowned. "It's not that chilly to me."

"No, I'm fine." Caitlin looked behind at Alex and he had the nerve to wink at her. Quickly, she turned back to Hallie. "Why don't you ride Red Fire? He's okay now that the dog is gone."

Hallie's expression brightened. "But I thought you said I wasn't ready to ride in the pasture yet."

"Well, your dad and I are right here. You can just ride him back to the barn and we'll walk beside you." That way Alex could keep one hand on the gelding's bridle, just in case. "I'll lean on my horse instead of you. How would that be?"

"Sweet!" Hallie stopped in her tracks. "Can I, Dad?"

"I suppose."

Caitlin ignored the look he gave her. A look that

said he was still apprehensive after what had just happened, and also said he wanted her to lean on him again. Wanted to wrap his arm around her waist. And she foolishly wanted the same thing.

Yet Alex might want more from her than she could honestly give him. The thought of him seeing her scarred body made her nauseous. But they could be friends, like he'd said.

"Go on," Caitlin said to Hallie. "Your dad can give you a leg up, and I'll stand right here and hold your backpack."

Alex had halted nearby, holding on to Red Fire. Hallie shrugged out of the backpack, then walked eagerly toward the horse. Her dad held his hands out with fingers laced, boosting her into the saddle.

"Wow, this feels weird after riding western," she said. "But I like it." She grinned, nudging the horse into a walk.

Alex strode along beside her, pausing to reach out to Caitlin. "Here, let me take that."

She handed him the backpack, then said to Hallie, "It's good to know how to ride both western and English. That leaves you able to participate in more events if you want to."

"Events?" Hallie's eyebrows rose. "You mean I might really be able to show or barrel race someday?"

"Sure. I thought that's why we were teaching you to ride."

Her face lit up. "Oh, my God! I can't wait to tell Jeanette, the girl I met at the dance."

Caitlin smiled, noticing the effect his daughter's happiness had on Alex. She was glad she could help brighten their day. Glad she'd taken a ride on Red Fire, even if it hadn't ended so well.

CHAPTER NINE

CAITLIN WOKE UP early Monday morning to a freak blizzard. For the first week of October, the storm was unusual. "Good grief, it looks like Christmas," Caitlin said to Spike as she slipped into a warm bathrobe and looked out the window. The little dog was none too happy to have to go outside and do his business in a half foot of snow. Leaving him in the backyard for a few minutes, she dressed in a sweater, jeans and hiking boots, then threw on her coat and went outside to feed the horses. Both geldings were waiting in their stalls, and Caitlin fed them each an extra flake of hay and a little more sweet feed to compensate for their body heat working overtime in the colder temperature. The barn thermostat read thirty degrees. Not terribly cold, but a far cry from last week's Indian summer days in the mid-sixties. But then, that was Colorado for you. If you didn't like the weather, just wait a minute.

With the horses fed, Caitlin hurried back into the house to give Spike his breakfast, shower, then make herself some raisin toast and oatmeal. She heard the school bus grinding up the road and looked out the kitchen window to see Hallie climb on board, with a coat over her jeans, wool hat and gloves. If the kid was game later, this could be her first chance to ride in the snow. Something Caitlin had always loved to do.

She rubbed her fingers against her left thigh as she sat with her bowl of oatmeal. Her escapade with Red Fire and the stray dog two days ago had left her stiff and achy, and the sudden change in weather wasn't helping any. With therapy scheduled for this morning, she hoped the snow stopped soon.

But by midmorning, the weather forecaster's dire predictions had changed her plans. Twelve inches of snow had already fallen, and more was expected. A travel advisory had been issued, people cautioned to stay home if at all possible. The phone rang and Caitlin picked up.

Her mom greeted her, then said, "I don't think we should go out in this storm, honey."

"I don't, either." Caitlin shivered, though not from the weather. No matter how hard she tried, she still couldn't shake memories of the accident. The thought of driving in a blizzard left her icy cold. "I'll call and reschedule."

By lunchtime, several more inches of snow lay on the ground, and still the flakes came down. She fixed herself a cup of tea and sat at the window, looking out at the scene in front of her. When was the last time she'd noticed what a postcard-perfect town she lived in? She'd always been so busy, going to college, traveling the show circuit.... She hadn't taken much time for the here and now.

She craned her neck to catch a glimpse of Alex's house. She could just make out the front end of his Ranger. It lay covered in snow, and she wondered what he was doing at that precise moment. Having coffee? Lunch? Was he thinking about her?

"Look at me," Caitlin said, stroking Spike's ears as the dog jumped up into her lap. "Snowbound for one morning, and already I'm going batty."

She took another sip of tea and gazed out over the pasture. Buried in a blanket of untouched white, it looked like a giant, downy quilt.

She couldn't remember the last time she'd felt so alone. Picking up a Sherrilyn Kenyon novel, she opened it to the bookmarked page. But the handsome hero in the story was enough to send her fantasies into overdrive. She sighed.

Surely it was only the weather.

ALEX PACED in front of the television. He'd almost called the school twice. He didn't want Hallie riding home on the bus. Didn't want his little girl's life entrusted to a stranger's driving skills. But he also didn't want to embarrass her by phoning the school.

Hello, would you please wrap my daughter in a warm blanket and tuck her in a safe place until I can come rescue her? Thank you.

Hallie would never speak to him again. He knew he could make it in the Ranger, with its four-wheel drive. He was used to driving in the mountains. He and Hallie had gone camping with Vince, D'Ann and Melissa on numerous occasions.

He glared at the telephone as if it were to blame. "Screw it." He strode to the end table and yanked out the phone book. If Hallie got upset, oh well. She'd get over it.

Alex had just laid his hand on the cordless when it rang, nearly startling him out of his skin. "Yeah?"

"Dad?"

"Hallie." His heart leaped. "What's wrong?"

"Nothing. God, are you all right?"

He took a deep breath. "Yeah, honey, I'm fine. I was just watching the weather report. Looks like we've got quite a storm on our hands."

"I know. Isn't it awesome?" Delight laced her tone, rubbing off on him, calming his nerves. Somewhat. "They're closing school early. But the buses can't make it that far out of town, so we're supposed to call our parents and make other arrangements. Jeanette's already called her mom, and she said I can stay at her house overnight if it's all right with you. They're not expecting school to be open tomorrow, either."

Alex had met Jeanette and her father at the dance. He was a local postal carrier, had lived in Deer Creek his entire life, and the Platzes' house was four blocks from the school.

"—and we can walk to her house," Hallie was saying.

"No!" The word came out, quick and sharp before he could stop it.

"What? Why not?" Hallie's voice became an angry whine.

"You can stay at Jeanette's," he quickly amended, "but I don't want you walking."

Dad, can Melissa and I walk down to the 7-Eleven? It's only three blocks.

A humming started inside his head, and the metallic taste of adrenaline filled his mouth.

He sank into a chair.

"—not a baby, Dad. God!"

"Hallie, the snow's two and a half feet deep."

"I've got my boots. And a coat. Come on, Dad. Please?"

He willed his heart to stop racing. "All right. But call me the minute you get to the Platzes' house, you hear?"

"I will. Thanks!"

"What about—" He started to ask about a toothbrush and a change of clothes, but she'd already hung up. Alex sat staring at the phone for a moment, then put it back on its base.

In the kitchen, he poured himself a cup of coffee and waited for the phone to ring again. The minutes on the clock ticked by. One felt like five. Two felt like thirty. A half hour later he was going nuts. Why the hell hadn't he asked for the Platzes' number? Damn it, he'd been so caught up in worrying, he'd overlooked the obvious. Hopefully they were listed in the book.

At the blare of the phone he grabbed for the receiver. "Hello?"

"Sorry, Dad. I almost forgot to call you. Mrs. Platz had hot chocolate with whipped cream waiting. And double-fudge-chunk cookies."

He closed his eyes and let out a breath he'd held for what seemed an eternity. "You made it then."

"Duh. I've got to go. Mrs. Platz is expecting a phone call."

"Wait." He grabbed a pen and paper. "Give me their number." A minute later, he hung up, feeling relieved. Sort of.

He knew he had to let his daughter go places and have fun. She needed to be with friends, and he was glad to see her behaving like a regular kid. Still, part of him wished Hallie were safe at home, tucked into her own room with a cup of instant cocoa he'd made, with the mini marshmallows she liked so much.

"Okay, I made the effort," he said out loud. "I'm trying." He went to the window and looked out at the snow. Would it ever stop? He hadn't seen this much since the blizzard of 1982, when he was in elementary school. The school had closed then, too, and he and his buddies had run their sleds up and down the hill behind his best friend's house.

Yeah, snow was a good thing for a kid. He thought of Caitlin. How was she faring in this weather? Would she be able to feed her horses? She was still using her cane, and that might make it tricky. And the storm would cause darkness to come early. Maybe he should call her and find out if she needed help.

He started to move to the phone, then remembered how proud and stubborn she could be. No. He wouldn't call with the offer to lend a hand.

He would go over and insist on it.

Donning his cowboy hat, sheepskin-lined jacket and gloves, he made his way across the road. He could barely tell where the shoulder lay beneath the deep covering of snow. His jeans were caked with the stuff clear up to his knees by the time he stood on Caitlin's doorstep. Her walkway was covered, and it was hard to tell if she'd been outside at all.

He knocked, and when she answered he felt like he'd been hit with a snowball. In the head. Or maybe the stomach. She stood in the doorway in a hunter green sweater and black jeans, the breeze tugging her dark hair. She wasn't wearing any makeup, her long lashes blinking away the tiny snowflakes that blew in through the open door.

"Alex. What are you doing out in this weather? Come in." She held the door wide, and he stamped his boots off and brushed at the legs of his jeans with his gloved fingers before stepping inside.

"I thought you might need someone to shovel your walkway and feed your horses," he said. "Lord, where did this crazy weather come from?" The weatherman had predicted an early snow, but not this much.

"There's no point in shoveling," she said with a half laugh. "It'll just get buried again. And I can feed the horses myself, thanks. I did it this morning."

"Yeah, but the snow wasn't this deep then." He looked at her cane, then jerked his gaze away, silently cursing himself.

"So? I may be short, but I'm not that short." She gave him a wry smile. "I won't sink in above my head if that's what you're worried about."

Her leveled chin challenged him to state the real reason for his concern. "I know you're capable," he said, groping lamely for something that didn't sound just that—lame. "But I'm going nuts cooped up in that house with nothing to do. So why not let me help?"

"Don't you have work to do?"

Busted. "Yeah, but who wants to sit at the computer on a day like this?" He gave her his best flirty grin. "Don't you know even big boys like to play in the snow?" And that fast, he could picture the two of them chasing each other in the snow. Throwing snowballs.

"...no need, really, Alex. You might as well go home. I heard on the news they were closing the schools. Don't you have to pick up Hallie, or is the bus going to make it out here?"

"She's staying at a friend's house for the night, a few blocks from the school. So she's safe and warm."

"Glad to hear it. But I'm fine. Really."

"Why do you have to be so stubborn?" he asked.

"I'm not the one who's stubborn," she returned. She opened her mouth to say something more, but the ringing phone cut her off. "Excuse me."

Alex tried not to eavesdrop, but he couldn't help it.

"No, Mother, I'm fine. No, Dillon doesn't need to try to come out here in this storm. I'll manage. Yes." She rolled her eyes, the gesture so similar to Hallie's he had to smother a chuckle. "No. Mother, that's not necessary." Her voice rose. "I don't—"

"Allow me." Impulsively, Alex took the phone away from her, ignoring her indignant gasp and the heated look she gave him. "Mrs. Kramer? Alex Hunter here. Yeah." He paused, listening, barely focused on Evelyn Kramer's words. Instead, he watched Caitlin's pretty blue eyes flash fire at him. "I plan to help Caitlin with her chores. As a matter of fact, I'm going to do them for her, and she can sit right here by the fire and sip hot chocolate. Yeah. You're welcome." He handed the phone back to Caitlin, his eyes innocently wide.

She snatched it from his grasp and he laughed. *Oh, this was fun.*

"Why did you do that?" she said in a stage whisper. She spoke to her mother again, then glared at him after hanging up.

"Do what? Help you get your mom and your brother off your back?"

She started to protest, then clamped her mouth shut. "All right. I guess you've got a point. But I can handle my own problems, thank you very much." She sank onto the couch.

Alex opened the door of the wood-burning stove. He checked the flue and eyed the small pile of firewood in the wood box. "That won't last long, but it'll do for now." He found some newspaper in the bottom of the box and crumpled it to stuff into the bottom of the stove. He glanced over his shoulder at Caitlin as he stacked wood inside. "Aren't you going to offer me some coffee?"

"Coffee? You step in here and take over my life and you want me to give you coffee?"

He shrugged. "Sure. It's cold out there, and I'll need something to warm me up if I'm going to go out and shovel a path for your dog."

"What?" She let out an involuntary laugh.

"Yeah." He pointed at Spike. "Poor little dog, he'll get lost in those drifts."

Caitlin shook her head. "You're too much." But she rose from the couch. "I don't drink coffee. Will tea or hot chocolate do?"

"Hot chocolate." He grinned at her, loving the way she looked when she got all riled. "But I might as well go out and shovel first, since I'm already wet. I'll take the cocoa when I get back inside." He got the fire started, then moved to the front door, pausing with his hand on the knob. "Where's your snow shovel?"

"I don't have one. I wasn't expecting winter yet."

"And you were going to clear your own walkway…how?"

She flushed. "I wasn't. I was just going to walk through the snow." She waved her hand casually. "Or use the scoop shovel from the barn."

He grunted. "I'll get my snow shovel. Be right back."

Within a short time, he had an area cleared in the yard for Spike to use, and the walkway to the barn. Sweat beaded his forehead in spite of the cold, and he wiped it away with one gloved hand, leaning on the shovel for a moment to take in the view.

"It's pretty, isn't it?" Caitlin said as she walked up behind him.

"Yeah, it is. A far cry from Denver."

The sky had turned a faded charcoal. The snow-flakes were reduced to tiny specks of white, like minute down feathers falling to the ground. But the wind was nasty.

Caitlin shivered. "It's getting colder. You'd better come in for that hot chocolate." She called to Spike, who'd hurriedly done his business.

The three of them climbed the porch steps, and Alex dusted the snow from his hat, then once again stamped his feet and brushed off his jeans.

"You're all wet," Caitlin said once they'd entered the living room. "Why don't you sit by the fire and warm up."

"Sounds good to me." He sank into a chair in front of the woodstove, and stretched his legs out to let the heat dry his jeans. Caitlin brought him a cup of hot chocolate—no marshmallows. He tasted it and grimaced. "What is this?"

"Sugar-free cocoa with low-fat milk." She shrugged, sitting on the nearby couch. "It's better for you."

"What are you, some kind of a health nut?"

She graced him with a thin smile. "I told you. I like to take care of my body so I can…" her smile vanished "…so I can ride." She let her hands fall into her lap. "Guess it's not so important anymore, is it?"

"Nonsense. You rode." A laugh slipped out. "Sort of."

Caitlin found herself laughing, too. "Yeah, I guess I did, if that's what you want to call it."

"Hey, look at it this way. You might've come up with a new rodeo event."

"Very funny," she growled, but her eyes lit up.

Spike jumped into his lap and gave Alex's hands a washing with his tongue, while he patted the dog. "Hey, fella. Are you thanking me for shoveling out your yard? Huh?" He ruffled the dog's ears. "He's cute."

"Sometimes." Caitlin spoke with affection. "Sometimes he's a pain in the butt. Comes with the breed."

"Well, Hallie sure likes him."

"Maybe you ought to get her a puppy."

"And have all my boots and shoes chewed to ribbons? No thanks."

"How about an older dog?"

He pursed his lips, nodding. "Might not be a bad idea. I really hadn't thought past the horse. Speaking of which, I was just about finished with the arena over at my place, and the repairs on the barn, when this snow hit." He got up and moved to sit on the end of the couch opposite her. "You sure you don't mind Hallie coming over all the time to be with Red Fire? I don't want her pestering you."

"She's not a pest. I like her."

"Sometimes I think she gets a little lonely, being an only child. She misses her cousin."

"I'll bet she does." Caitlin's voice was soft. "So, how come you never remarried and had more kids?"

He shrugged, not wanting to admit his distrust of women. "Between work and raising Hallie, I never made much time for socializing. How about you?"

She looked as if he'd suggested she wear a bikini in the blizzard. "You mean have I had a serious relationship?"

"Yeah." He knew there couldn't be a man in her life at the moment. Otherwise, where was he? But what he didn't understand was, why not?

She shook her head. "I guess I've gone a similar route to yours. Except it was school and riding that took my focus."

Alex studied her profile. She was so temptingly beautiful. He couldn't believe she didn't realize it.

"What?" Caitlin looked at him.

He arched his eyebrows and shook his head. "Nothing."

"You were staring."

"Was I?"

"Yes." She glowered at him. "Something on your mind?"

If she only knew. "Nothing, really. I was just thinking. I don't know much about you."

"What do you want to know?"

He smiled. "You haven't told me what you plan to do now that you won't be riding in the Olympics."

Her expression sobered. "I don't know yet. I suppose I'll eventually go back to school."

"School?"

"I was in my final year at Colorado State before the crash."

He did the math. "I thought you'd already graduated."

"I took a year off to ride the show circuit in Europe. Otherwise, I would've graduated last year."

"Europe. Wow. I've barely been out of the state."

She cuddled a pillow against her stomach, tucking her stocking feet underneath her. "You ought to travel. It's fun seeing the world."

"Yeah, well it's a little hard to do when you're a single parent." He wished he had the money to take a trip with Hallie to Europe. Or Australia. "I did, however, take Hallie to Disneyland when she was eight. And Six Flags Over Texas when she was ten."

"Nothing wrong with that." She smiled. "I like amusement parks, too."

"Really?"

She smiled without humor. "Of course, if I was to get on a roller coaster now, I'd probably end up with motion sickness."

"How long do the doctors think it will take for your head injury to completely heal?"

She shrugged. "They're not sure. It may never get any better. But I've come a long way, so I'm not giving up yet."

"That's the spirit."

She grimaced. "Yeah, well, it's hard to keep positive all the time."

She revealed the depth of her vulnerability in those few words. He knew how hard losing her equestrian career had been, and how much it obviously meant to her. But he was getting a better picture of what she must go through on a daily basis—what she had already gone through.

Impulsively, he reached out and touched her cheek. "No one expects you to be perfect, Caitlin," he said softly.

Her blue eyes met his. "I've always been a perfectionist. Like I told you, for me it's all or nothing."

He lowered his hand. "So if you only make an eighty or ninety percent recovery, that's not good enough?" He thought of Melissa. If she would've lived, it wouldn't have mattered what other damage the bullet had done.

Caitlin squeezed the pillow tighter. "I'm grateful for every single day. For every step forward in my recovery. And I know that there are a lot of people far worse off than I am." She lifted her hands. "But I still can't help the way I feel, Alex. I want what I had before. And if I can't have that, I know I'll never be completely satisfied."

"Why do I get the impression you don't mean to be selfish?"

"Selfish?" She looked appalled, then contrite. "Jeez. I guess I could sound that way. I'm just hard on myself. I always have been."

"Really?" He grinned. "I never would have guessed."

She smacked him with the pillow. "Speaking of which, I have no intention of sitting in here sipping hot chocolate while you do my chores." She rose from the couch. "You can help, but I'm going out, too. And I think I'll feed early, before the temperature drops any lower." She moved to the window and looked out. "The snow's almost stopped—finally. If the cloud cover dissipates, it'll be freezing out there in no time."

"I really don't mind, Caitlin. It'll only take a few minutes to feed two horses."

She slipped her hiking boots on. "Then it'll take half that with two of us."

Damned, but she was stubborn. "Suit yourself." He slipped his coat on, then held the door for her.

The icy wind hit him as soon as he stepped outside.

Caitlin shivered, hunkering her shoulders against the squall. "Let's hurry."

He took her cane from her and held out his elbow. "Here, allow me. It'll be easier this way."

She hesitated, then slipped her hand through his arm, and her touch made him forget about the wind.

"Thanks."

"My pleasure." He tipped his hat in an exaggerated cowboy style, then shot her a grin.

She laughed, and the wind caught the sound and carried it away. It blew her hair in a fluffy toss of chocolate-brown. She should have worn a hat. But she looked so damned pretty, her cheeks pink, the snow around her all white and pure.

Alex couldn't help himself. He pulled her around to face him, his arms circling her waist. "You're beautiful," he said.

"What?" she gasped, bracing her hands against him, her breath blowing out in a white plume. "Alex, it's freezing out here. I think your brain has gone numb."

"There's nothing wrong with my brain," he said. "Or my eyesight, either." He held her with his arms looped around her waist. "I could look at you like this all day." With the snow in her hair, her lips a bright rose. He wanted to taste them. Taste her.

She shifted in obvious discomfort. "You don't have to say that."

He frowned. "I know that." He craned his neck to look both ways, then gave an exaggerated smirk. "Nope. Nobody twisting my arm."

"Alex." She laughed, and the sound warmed him.

"Yeah?" His heart raced.

"Yeah," she whispered. Then she leaned into him and kissed him.

CHAPTER TEN

CAITLIN CLOSED her eyes and focused on the sweet taste of Alex's lips on hers—his tongue in her mouth—and groaned. She'd missed being held, kissed. Missed the feel of a man's strong arms around her. Ignoring the wind and cold, she enjoyed the sheer pleasure that filled her as they kissed again and again.

"Caitlin," he murmured. He deepened the kiss. Pressing one hand to the nape of her neck, he put the other on the small of her back. Her arms looped around his neck, she drew herself even closer, sliding her hips up against his.

And slipped on the ice.

Enough to throw her hip out of whack. With a cry, she pulled away from Alex.

"Are you all right?" He studied her, looking down in concern.

Embarrassed, Caitlin suddenly felt the sharp sting of the wind, and the pain in her hip as she rubbed at her cramped muscles. Worst of all, she felt humiliated.

Hell, she couldn't even kiss right.

"I'm fine." She stepped back. "I—just got a muscle cramp." She tucked her hair behind one ear, lowering her gaze. "Must've stepped wrong on the ice. I'm sorry." She turned toward the barn, but he caught her by the elbow.

"Caitlin, wait." He frowned. "What's the matter?"

"Nothing." She met his gaze. "I shouldn't have done that. I'm sorry."

"I'm not."

"Well, I am. I shouldn't have kissed you." She lifted her shoulders. "So let's just forget it ever happened." She took a couple of unsteady steps toward the barn before Alex cupped her elbow, steadying her.

Damn it, what had he done with her cane?

"Hold up a minute."

"No, it's cold." She slid the barn door open and stepped inside.

Alex closed it behind them. "Caitlin, what's the matter?" He halted her once more with a touch to her arm. "Did I do something to offend you?"

She clamped her jaw shut to stop from shaking. The sweet, heavy odor of the hay reminded her how much fun it was to make out with a good-looking guy on a blanket in the barn. And she knew it would be ten times better with Alex.

If only she'd met him before the crash.

"No, you didn't do anything." She made her voice sound casual. "I told you, I shouldn't have kissed you. That's all."

"Why not?"

"Because." She glared at him. "I don't want to get involved with you, Alex, okay?"

The hurt in his eyes struck her in the pit of the stomach, but she stood her ground. Better now than later.

"You don't have to hit me with a sledgehammer." He reached for a bale of hay. From his pocket, he took a knife and sliced the nylon baling twine.

Caitlin wanted to apologize, but she couldn't. She would only make things worse. She took a couple of flakes of hay and tossed them to Silver Fox as he shifted about in his stall, nickering softly. "You hungry, boy?" She got him another two flakes, then added some grain.

Silent, Alex fed Red Fire. When they finished, he shut the barn door, then took her arm so she didn't fall as they went back to the house, careful to keep a respectful distance between them. He walked her to the door but made no move to come in.

"Aren't you going to come in?"

"I need to get home."

"Oh." She couldn't let him leave like that. She didn't want him to think he'd done something wrong. Didn't want to be rude to him after all the nice things he'd done for her. "Are you sure? Because I really would like to talk to you for a minute. Please?"

Before he could answer, the phone rang. *Damn.* Caitlin held the door wide. "Let me grab that. Come on in." She hurried to answer the cordless without giving him the chance to say no.

"Hello?"

"This is Sandy Platz. I'm calling for Hallie Hunter. She thought her father might be there at your house."

"Yes, he is. Just a moment, please." She handed the phone to Alex, who'd shut the door behind him but still stood in front of it. "For you."

"Me?" Puzzled, he took the cordless. "Hello?" His expression became worried as he listened. "Is she running a fever? Maybe I ought to come get her.... Are you sure? Well, all right. Can you put her on the phone?" He spoke to Hallie for a few minutes, then hung up and handed the phone back to Caitlin.

"Everything all right?"

"Hallie's sick."

"Oh, no."

"Mrs. Platz said she'd been throwing up. But she doesn't seem to be running a fever."

"That's too bad—that she's sick, I mean." Caitlin frowned. "She got sick last week at the Sadie Hawkins dance, too."

"What do you mean?" The line in Alex's forehead deepened.

"In the bathroom. She was vomiting, but she said she'd had too much junk food."

"Well, apparently that wasn't the case. She's been acting a little off lately. I'll bet she's caught a flu bug."

"Probably, with this weird weather we're having." She recalled Hallie's flushed appearance that night.

"I'd really like to get her, but like Sandy said, the roads are treacherous." Alex chewed his bottom lip, shifting his weight.

"She's right. And as long as Hallie isn't running a fever, there's not much you can do for her that Sandy can't."

"What if she gets worse and needs to see a doctor?"

Caitlin shrugged. "Then she's better off being in town right now, closer to the hospital. You could always have Sandy drive her and meet her there."

"That's true," he agreed, but his tone was reluctant.

His concern for his daughter touched Caitlin, and she felt bad for having hurt his feelings moments ago. "Are you sure you wouldn't like to stay for another cup of hot chocolate?"

He shook his head. "Thanks, but I think I'll go on home. That way I'll be right by the phone if Hallie needs me."

Caitlin didn't argue the point that Hallie had found him just fine. "Well, thanks again for helping me feed."

"Anytime." He moved to the door. "If you need anything, don't hesitate to call."

Then he was gone. And that quick, the house was quiet and empty.

Too quiet and empty. Caitlin sighed and sank onto the sofa with Spike. "What am I going to do, boy?" she asked, scratching the little dog behind the ears.

She couldn't win for losing. Alone, she felt miserable, and with someone, she felt inadequate. She curled her hand over the arm of the couch, where Alex's own had rested a short while ago. Sitting where he'd sat. She thought she could detect the faint scent of whatever cologne or aftershave it was he wore. Reminding her of how good it had felt to have him here. Laughing, talking. Kissing her.

Her cheek against the back of the couch, Caitlin inhaled. She leaned her head back, closed her eyes and remembered Alex's lips on hers. Recalled the hot, sweet taste of his tongue.

Empty cup in hand, Caitlin rose. Pausing in front of the mirror hanging near the doorway of the small dining area, she wrinkled her nose at her reflection.

What did she want?

What *did* she plan to do with the rest of her life? She truly didn't have an answer.

ALEX MANAGED to hold off calling Sandy's house for all of thirty minutes. Sandy reassured him Hallie seemed to be feeling fine. Still he asked to speak to her.

"Hello?"

"Don't sound so suspicious," he said. "I just wanted to make sure you're feeling okay."

"Dad, I'm fine. Jeez. You don't have to make a big fuss."

"All right, all right. I just wanted to be certain."

"Okay. Can I go now?"

"Sure, honey. Don't forget to thank Mrs. Platz for letting you stay."

"I will. Bye." She hung up, the dial tone humming in his ear.

Alex set the phone down. *Two for two.* In less than ten minutes, he'd managed to tick off both the women in his life. What was he talking about? Caitlin wasn't in his life.

He grabbed a can of Pepsi from the fridge to wash away the taste of that crap she called cocoa. But all he could taste in his mind, on his lips, was Caitlin.

Alex slouched into his recliner. What the hell had made her react that way? She'd seemed to be as into the kiss as he was, then all of a sudden she'd turned as cold as the wind blowing around them.

He clicked on the television. *Women.* Who could figure them out? He was done trying.

He went to bed early and tossed and turned, still worried about Hallie. Sure, she'd said she was fine, but why was it she'd gotten sick at the dance, too?

That had been over a week ago. Maybe it was just a coincidence.

He woke up the next morning at six-thirty, showered and dressed. The local radio station reported the ten-degree temperature, and the fact that the schools were still closed. Hallie would be thrilled.

Should he go over to Caitlin's and feed her horses? Or would that irritate her? She was so damned stubborn. He looked outside at the gray beginnings of morning. The snow had stopped last night, but the plow had yet to come through.

Alex put his boots on, still undecided. On the one hand, he didn't want to appear pushy. After all, if Caitlin really didn't want his help, that was her business. But on the other, since Hallie was using her horse, he felt an obligation to help with the care of the animal, seeing as how Hallie wasn't here to do it herself. His mind made up, he donned coat and hat and went outside.

Caitlin's house was dark, other than the yard light out back. It shone across the road between their houses, casting a glow on the single set of tire tracks marring the expanse of white, where someone had braved their way through the storm. He hoped the snowplow came by soon. He wanted to pick up Hallie.

The horses weren't in the paddock or pasture as far as he could see. They nickered to him from their stalls when he slid the barn door open. He found the light switch and, speaking to the geldings conversationally, fed them their morning rations. The stock tank outside had a heater in it to keep ice from forming, but he checked the water level to be sure they had plenty.

Outside once more, he hesitated, glancing at the house. Still no lights. Caitlin must be sleeping in. He didn't blame her. He wouldn't mind crawling back under the covers himself.

He returned to his house, got a cup of coffee and sat at his desk to work on one of his computer games. Engrossed in a phenomenal graphics program he'd recently begun using, he was startled to see it was already eight-thirty when he glanced up at the clock. A decent hour to call the Platzes.

Hallie grumbled when he told her he was coming to get her. But she had little choice, with Fred already gone and Sandy getting ready to head for work, since the roads in town had been plowed. Sandy was sending Jeanette to a neighbor's house to spend the day.

Alex hung up, noticing that the sun had begun to shine while he'd been busy at his desk. Outside, the blinding light sparkled off the glittering snow, making him duck his head, hat brim shielding his eyes. He climbed behind the wheel of his pickup and turned the key in the ignition. It clicked once and gave a dull half turn, then nothing.

"Damn it." He tried again with no luck. Alex slammed his palms against the steering wheel. He hated to, but it looked like he would have to ask Caitlin if he could borrow her truck.

Pocketing his keys, Alex was about to head across the road when he saw a lone figure coming his way.

Caitlin. And she looked pissed.

CAITLIN CROSSED the road as carefully, yet as quickly as she could. It wouldn't do to storm after Alex only to slip and fall on her butt.

"Hey there, sleepyhead." He gave her that crooked grin in an obvious attempt to disarm her.

"That's not going to work, Alex," she said. And before he could open his mouth again added, "Save the 'Aw, shucks, ma'am' routine for someone else."

His grin faded. "You're mad because I fed your horses."

"Bingo."

"Why?"

"My God, what does it take to get through to you? You're worse than my brother."

To her annoyance, he laughed. "I'll take that as a compliment."

"I wouldn't."

"Look, I fed your horses because one of them is

Hallie's responsibility now, and she's not here. You were obviously asleep, and I have to go out anyway to pick her up, so I figured, why not?"

How could she argue with that? "Fine. Thanks."

"Oh, please. Don't be so syrupy sweet."

"Very funny."

"Where's your cane?"

"What?"

"Your cane." He gestured.

Caitlin lifted her arms and looked down at her feet. "I don't have it." She looked at him.

"No." A smile tugged at the corners of his mouth. "I'd say not."

"I left it in the barn." She'd been so ticked off when she'd seen Silver Fox and Red Fire already munching hay, she'd forgotten the cane she'd leaned against the haystack.

His grin spread and a chuckle rumbled in his chest. "Don't look so shocked. I knew you could do it sooner or later."

"Then why have you been treating me like an invalid?" Pride would not let her irritation fade that quickly.

"I haven't been," he said quietly. "I've been treating you like a friend."

You don't kiss your friends. Not like that.

"Speaking of which, I need a favor from you."

"Oh?"

"My truck won't start, and I have to go get Hallie. Any chance I can borrow yours?"

Having the shoe suddenly on the other foot left her speechless for a full two seconds. "Sure." She shrugged. "I can't drive it yet anyway." She gave a small laugh. "Boy, that didn't come out very nice, did it?" Suddenly she felt ashamed of herself for being so hard on him. He really was a good guy.

Not to mention a good kisser.

"I knew what you meant."

"Okay. Let me get the keys." She started back across the road, and the knowledge that she really didn't have her cane to lean on began to fully sink in. Doubt shook her, and she found herself slowing, walking stiltedly—arms out—certain she would slip and fall.

Fall and further humiliate herself.

"Here. Let me help you, Ms. Independent."

Alex had come up beside her, his footsteps quiet in the deep snow. He took her arm before she could protest, and the familiar gesture warmed her.

She didn't protest. She simply let him lead her to the house. "I'll get your cane," he said, and left before she could reply.

Caitlin hurried inside, dodging Spike as he jumped in the air, begging to go with her. "We're not going anywhere, Spike." But he danced harder when he spotted the truck keys. "I'm just getting my keys. Silly dog."

Outside, she handed the keys to Alex and took her cane.

"Good thing I cut that baling twine off your driveshaft," he said. "Have you started it since then?"

"No."

"Okay. It might be a little cold-blooded, but we'll get 'er." He stood beside the Chevy. "Wanna go with me?"

She looked around at the snow and shivered. Not with cold. "No, thanks. By the way, how is Hallie feeling this morning?"

"Seems to be fine. At least, she sounded okay when I talked to her."

"That's good." She stood there a moment longer, wanting to accept his invitation, yet not quite ready for a drive in the snow.

The first since her accident.

Suddenly, Alex burst into laughter, his gaze on something behind her. "What?" Caitlin turned to look over her shoulder, and saw Spike in the window. He stood on top of the back of the couch, then sprang from there to the cushions and up again. His toenails scraped the windowpane as he whined and danced on his hind legs, ears flat, body wriggling.

"I'd say somebody wants to go for a ride." Alex grinned.

Her heart melted, and so did her apprehension.

"It might be nice to get out for a while."

His eyes told her he understood. "Nothing like a drive in a winter wonderland."

Caitlin rolled her tongue against her cheek. "Gee, cowboy, I didn't know you were so poetic."

"I try. I'll warm up the truck while you get your dog."

Within minutes they were on the road. Caitlin had opted to leave her cane at home, since she'd managed to cross the road without it and didn't plan to do much walking. It felt good not to have its presence in the pickup's cab with her. And it felt even better to ride down the snowy back roads with Alex, Spike on her lap with his paws braced against the window. Ears perked, he looked out, watching the passing scenery.

Caitlin thought she'd feel tense traveling through the snow-clogged roads. But the sun was out and the temperature was already on its way up. Halfway to town, they passed a snowplow. The driver waved and continued on his way, and the Chevy rolled onto the cleared area, traveling steadily along. Alex turned toward the two-lane highway.

"Where are you going?"

He looked at her, puzzled. "To town."

"I always take the frontage road."

"Yeah, but I figure the snowplows will have the highway well cleared. It'll be quicker and easier."

"That's true." She gripped the armrest, her knuckles white.

"Something wrong?"

"Not really." She felt foolish. It was just a road after all.

"Caitlin. What is it?"

She sighed. "The wreck was on this road," she said. "Up ahead, just before you reach town. I normally avoid driving past there."

He mumbled an expletive. "Why didn't you say something?" He slowed the Chevy but the snow-banked road offered no place to safely turn around.

"No, Alex, don't." She laid her hand on his arm. There wasn't very much traffic in the aftermath of the storm, still, trying to make a U-turn wouldn't be safe. She pictured another car, coming around a bend, hitting them. Sending the Chevy flying. Her heart raced.

"I can find a driveway to turn into."

"No. Really. Just…go. I'll be fine."

"Okay." He shrugged, apprehensive.

She stroked Spike's back, taking comfort from the dog's warm presence. Alex was a good driver. An excellent driver, in fact. He handled the Chevy on the slick roads easily. And they were traveling at a slow speed. Safe.

A mile went by, then another. They drew closer to the bend in the road where she'd had the flat tire that night. Where Amanda Kelly had pulled her Blazer over to lend a hand, and had paid for it big-time.

And then, they were there. Caitlin sucked in her breath and looked over at the shoulder.

"Stop the car," she said.

"What?"

"The truck." She waved her hand. "Stop the truck, Alex, please."

He glanced at her as though she were nuts, but he managed to find a place to pull over where the plow hadn't piled up too much snow.

Making Spike stay in the pickup, Caitlin got out and stood at the edge of the road. The distant sound of traffic reached her ears. On the opposite side, from the river in the ravine below, a bird called.

But Caitlin focused only on one thing. Cautiously, looking both ways first, she crossed the road and climbed over the foot-high snowbank left by the plows, stumbling, catching herself with her hand.

"Caitlin!" Alex called. "What in the hell are you doing?"

She heard him get out of the truck.

But she didn't answer. Didn't turn to look back at him.

All she could do was stare at the memorial wreath, pink-and-white silk rosebuds woven around a white cross...partially buried beneath the snow.

The cross that marked the place where Amanda Kelly's unborn baby had died.

CHAPTER ELEVEN

NEVER FORGET.

The words on the wooden cross broke Caitlin's heart as she brushed the snow away. "It's not fair," she said, as Alex came up behind her. "He killed an unborn baby."

Alex put his hands on her shoulders. "I know. I read it in the article about your accident."

"Crash," she said. "That's what they call it at MADD—Mothers Against Drunk Driving. My mother's a member of the local chapter. Nikki Somers—the biological mother of the baby—is, too. Mom's talked to her a lot. Her sister, the one who was also hit by the drunk, was a surrogate for her. She nearly died, as well. It makes me so angry."

"I know how you feel. I wanted to get my hands on the boy who shot Melissa pretty bad."

"I'm sure you did. I'd like to pop Lester Godfrey upside the head myself." She laughed dryly. "Here I've been whining over my injuries and my riding career, and these people have to cope with the death of their baby. Makes me feel awfully petty."

He kissed her temple. "You're not being petty. We've all got our problems, our tragedies to deal with."

Without thinking, she covered his hands with hers, still gazing at the memorial wreath. Her eyes stung. "I didn't know this was here." They stood for a moment, silent.

He smoothed her hair. "You okay?"

"Yeah." She wiped her cheeks with both hands. "I need to take flowers to that baby's grave."

"Just say the word. I'll go with you anytime."

"Thanks." She sniffed. "Come on. We'd better go get Hallie." When they were back in the truck, Caitlin was quiet for a while, unable to get Nikki Somers and her baby off her mind. What would it be like to be a mother? To lose a child? She thought of Hallie, who had no mother. "You know, it might be fun for Hallie to go riding in the snow, if she feels up to it. I thought about it yesterday, when it first began to snow, but of course, I hadn't expected it to be this deep. Guess we'll have to wait until it melts off a little."

"With the sun out like this, it shouldn't take long. I'm sure she'd like that."

"If the weather stays nasty we can always take her over to Foxwood to ride. We've got an indoor arena, and I'm sure Dillon wouldn't mind hauling Red Fire."

"She'd like that, too. As long as she's on a horse, she's happy."

"I can relate."

"You know, I've been thinking it might be nice if I got myself a horse. That way I can ride with her on an animal I feel comfortable with." He chuckled.

"That's a good idea."

"Are there any quarter-horse ranches in the area?"

"Sure. There's one on County Road 311 outside of Ferguson, and another one out on Deer Valley Road, not far from your place. It's smaller, but they have some nice horses."

"You want to come along and show me where they are?"

She started to refuse, but she was sick and tired of being cooped up in the house. Giving Hallie riding lessons helped her stay busy, but she needed something more to do with her time. "All right. I can give you the phone numbers so you can call and make appointments."

"Sounds good, but I think I'll wait until the weather clears. Plus, I still have to finish the repairs on my barn."

She wanted to offer him the use of her barn for his horse, but she resisted. She needed to stop tormenting herself this way.

HALLIE SAT cross-legged on her bed doing homework. The teachers had piled on extra when they'd realized school would be closed for a day or two. But it was worth it to get out of going. She was glad the sun was out, and thrilled to know that once the drifts melted down, she could go for her first horseback ride in the snow.

"You okay, Hal?" Her dad stood in her bedroom doorway.

"Yeah. Just doing cruddy homework."

He laughed. "Glad to see you're feeling well enough to complain about it. Need anything? Some juice or something?"

"No. I'm fine."

"Okay, then. I'll leave you to it."

When he left, Hallie got up and closed her door, then turned on her stereo. She'd nearly blown it, binging and purging at Jeanette's house. Thank God Mrs. Platz thought it was the flu. Still, the woman had to go and call her dad and make a big deal out of it. *Shit.*

She needed to be more careful. But that was the problem. She'd known it wasn't a great idea to purge in the Platzes' bathroom—that someone might hear her—but she couldn't stop. Before, binging and purging were her key to control. Lately, however, she felt out of sorts.

As though the purging was now in control of her.

WITHIN THREE DAYS, the snow had completely melted as Indian summer once again returned to Colorado's western slope. Caitlin made an appointment to see her doctor and was thrilled to find she no longer needed to wear the back brace. A week later, she accompanied Alex and Hallie to the quarter-horse ranches she'd told him about, and he ended up buying a beautiful ten-year-old blue roan gelding. He'd finished up the repairs on his barn and the arena, and had moved Red Fire to his place, as well.

Since Caitlin no longer needed her cane, unless she did an extensive amount of walking, she was able to take care of Silver Fox with no trouble at all. Though she still gave Hallie riding lessons, they spent less time together now that Red Fire was at Alex's. He felt comfortable with his new horse and had been taking Hallie riding often, first in their pasture—he'd also installed a hot wire—and then on some nearby trails.

But by the time Halloween rolled around, the temperature turned cold again, and Caitlin found herself giving Hallie lessons in Foxwood's indoor arena as planned. She was now able to drive a little, but not well enough to go on the highway or pull a trailer. Her mother or Dillon took care of hauling Red Fire back and forth, and either her mother or Gran drove her to Glenwood Springs—twenty miles away—to her therapist.

November came with a flurry of snowstorms, followed by a cold spell, then sunshine. Caitlin took advantage of a day when the temperature was fairly mild to go for a walk. Both her therapist and orthopedist had recommended walking as a form of exercise, gradually building her strength and stamina as she increased the distance. With Spike on a leash, Caitlin set off down the road.

It was Saturday, and she had a riding lesson later with Hallie. They'd been working hard, preparing for an upcoming gymkhana. If the weather held, they'd be able to have today's lesson at Alex's place. His truck was parked in the driveway, and Caitlin hurried past, not wanting him to see her. She didn't want to be alone with him. To her relief, he hadn't brought up the kiss again. Yet she couldn't seem to get it off her mind.

An hour later, she returned from her walk, hip throbbing. The dull ache in her back made her long to stretch out on the couch with the heating pad. Maybe she'd sit down with a notebook and pen, and work out a game plan for her future. She needed to make up her mind about going back to school. She wanted her degree, but her original goal of majoring in animal science seemed pointless now. Of course, there were other ways to apply her studies. She could go back to class in January, after Christmas break, since she only needed a semester to get enough credits to graduate. Or she could wait until next summer or fall when she felt better.

If she felt better. She no longer relied on her cane,

but the pain never went away, and her energy still wasn't what it had once been.

As Caitlin neared home, she glanced across the road at Red Fire. It seemed odd to see him over there with Alex's gelding, Splash. She caught a glimpse of color in the tall weeds behind the barn, and realized it was Hallie. Even from this distance, Caitlin could see she was bent over, sick.

Frowning, she crossed the road. "Hallie, are you all right?"

The girl jumped. Hastily, she slipped something into her coat pocket—a spoon?—then wiped her hand across her mouth. "Caitlin. What are you doing here? It's not time for our lesson."

"No. I was coming back from a walk and I saw you." She studied Hallie's face. The girl looked tired, and her eyes were bloodshot. "You're sick again?"

"Yeah." Hallie shrugged. "It's nothing. I just can't seem to get rid of this flu bug." She gave a paper-thin smile. "Hope it's gone soon. My birthday's coming up the Friday before Thanksgiving, and Dad plans to take me out somewhere nice for dinner. Hey, you want to go with us?"

"Sure. If it's all right with your dad." It wouldn't be an actual date, since Hallie had been the one to invite her.

"Okay. I'll tell him." Hallie hurried away.

"Hallie," Caitlin called after her. "If you're sick, we can postpone your lesson."

"No, I'm okay. Riding always makes me feel better."

"All right, then. See you later." Caitlin lifted her hand in a wave.

In her kitchen, she fed Spike a dog biscuit and made herself a snack of low-fat Swiss cheese and a quartered apple. Surely Hallie hadn't carried a flu bug this long. What could be making her throw up all the time? A chill went through her. *Was she pregnant?* She wasn't even quite thirteen, but kids were having sex at ever younger ages these days. If Hallie had already gotten her period, then she was old enough to have a baby.

The thought mortified her. Should she say something to Alex? As Caitlin sat on the couch eating, another thought came to mind. Hallie was at an awkward age, when everything was magnified tenfold. An age when kids—especially girls—were under the constant scrutiny and pressure of their peers. She looked at the fashion magazine sitting on her coffee table, filled with photos of young, thin models, beautiful in their fashionable clothes—likely size four or smaller. These were the type of women that girls Hallie's age looked up to.

Everywhere you looked, the media bombarded you with the message to be thin. Low-carb this, diet plan that. Caitlin really hadn't thought a lot about her body size growing up, because she'd been taught by her mother and grandmother to eat right to stay in shape for riding. And the riding itself gave her plenty of exercise and muscle tone. She'd never had an issue with her weight because she'd never had a problem controlling it in a healthy manner.

But she knew women who did. Riders who suffered from the stress of wanting to be the best, always seeking a championship, a gold medal. Young women with parents who insisted on nothing less than first place. Every time. And often with the stress of living up to unreasonable expectations came eating disorders.

Was Hallie bulimic? Caitlin thought about the way she'd eaten large quantities of junk food at the Sadie Hawkins dance. And the big stack of pancakes the day Caitlin had breakfast with her and Alex. The girl had gone through a lot in her short life. No mother…the loss of her cousin in such a horrible way. Not to mention the fact that she'd witnessed the shooting. Caitlin shuddered. She'd been so wrapped up in her own problems, she hadn't given Hallie's more than a passing thought. Did Hallie's often moody exterior hide something more painful than normal teenage angst?

Caitlin picked up the phone to call Dillon. She had something in mind that would keep Hallie busy while she discussed this with Alex.

"HALLIE, are you ready?" Alex called.

"Yeah." She appeared in the bedroom doorway, dressed in jeans and a sweatshirt. "I'll go catch Red Fire."

Caitlin had called earlier and suggested a variation in Hallie's normal riding lesson. They'd go to the indoor arena at Foxwood Farms as they had before, but this time she'd be doing ground exercises that involved an obstacle course.

They met Caitlin in her driveway, since it was easier to navigate with the Kramers' large gooseneck trailer.

"Hi," she greeted them. "Dillon's with Dad at a horse show, so Mom's going to pick us up."

"That's nice of her," Alex said, "but I hate to bother your mom."

"She doesn't mind." She lowered her voice as Hallie led Red Fire over to the fence to greet Silver Fox. "As a matter of fact, I have something to talk to you about. I thought I'd let Mom show Hallie some exercises in the arena so we can have a few minutes alone."

"Okay." Puzzled, he contained his curiosity as Evelyn Kramer pulled into the driveway with the horse trailer in tow. After loading Red Fire, they piled in and made the short drive to Foxwood.

Hallie proudly saddled the gelding by herself once they arrived at the stables. "So, what are we going to do today?" she asked.

"I've set up some cavaletti for you," Evelyn said.

"What's that?"

"Ground rails. You trot over them. It not only keeps your horse alert—making him watch where he sets his feet—but it'll give you good practice in upper body position, rein release, leg position…things like that."

"Sounds complicated."

"It's not," Caitlin said. "Mom will show you."

"How come you're not going to?"

"Because—" Evelyn laid her hand on Hallie's shoulder "—I'm better at it." She laughed. "Actually, Caitlin and I thought you might benefit from watching me ride my horse, then follow along. Sound good?"

"Sure." Hallie mounted up and made her way with Evelyn down the walkway to the arena, where Evelyn's sorrel mare stood saddled and waiting.

Alex hung back, more than a little curious, until Hallie was out of earshot. "So, what's up?"

"Let's sit." Caitlin gestured for him to follow her to the bleachers. They climbed to the center row where they could talk privately, yet still have a good view of Hallie's progress. "I don't know how to tell you this."

"Just say it."

"Okay. Alex, I think your daughter has an eating disorder."

"What?" He drew back, certain she was kidding. "No way. Haven't you noticed the way she eats?"

"That's precisely what I'm talking about."

"Well, she's hardly anorexic. So, what do you mean?"

"Have you heard of bulimia?"

"Yeah. Sort of." He listened as she described the disease and rattled off her opinions on Hallie's eating habits. The more she talked, the madder he got. "Who the hell do you think you are?"

"Excuse me?"

He'd been afraid of Hallie getting hurt, but he'd never dreamed it would be in this way. "Why are you doing this, Caitlin? Why would you want to say such an ugly thing?"

She gaped at him. "Please keep your voice down. She'll hear you."

"Don't tell me what to do, or how to raise my daughter. You're insinuating I don't feed her properly?"

"That's not what I meant—"

"I don't need your opinion or your wild imagination."

"Alex, hear me out. I'm trying to help."

"I don't need your help, either."

"It's not normal to throw up like that for no reason."

"She's had the flu."

"For over a month?"

He turned away. "Look at her out there. She's

having fun. She's opened up more to you and these horses than I've seen her open up to anything or anyone in a long time."

"That's great. But it doesn't mean she doesn't have some underlying problems."

He counted to ten. "She doesn't have an eating disorder."

"I hope you're right. But I don't think so."

"Well, I don't give a damn what you think," he said, standing. "This conversation is over."

What the hell had gotten into the woman?

Alex hustled down the bleachers and leaned against the wall to watch Hallie ride through the cavaletti. Four poles made of PVC pipe, they'd been laid on the ground about four and a half feet apart to provide a pattern of obstacles. Having demonstrated on her mare, Evelyn now stood in the center of the arena, calling out instructions while Hallie worked her way—hesitantly at first—over the set of rails. The more she cantered around the arena, then slowed to trot over the rails, the more confident she grew. Red Fire knew what he was doing and soon settled into a familiar rhythm, which helped Hallie relax.

"You're doing great, Hal," Alex called, ignoring Caitlin.

Hallie grinned and kept riding. When she felt comfortable trotting over the rails, Evelyn raised the cavaletti six inches off the ground. Alex's heart flew into his throat as Red Fire jumped the first one, nearly shaking Hallie from the saddle. But she quickly righted herself.

"Easy does it," Evelyn instructed. "Eyes ahead. Hands still. That's the way."

Hallie balanced in the saddle, her face set in deep concentration.

Alex gripped the wall, tempted to put a stop to the lesson.

"That horse doesn't pose half the threat to her the bulimia does," Caitlin said in his ear.

He turned on her. "I told you. She's *not* bulimic." He spoke through gritted teeth, his voice low.

"Why don't you ask her?"

"Why don't you mind your own business?"

"Fine." She walked onto the floor to help Evelyn with the lesson.

Alex wanted to take his daughter home. But for her sake, he didn't make a scene. The hour-long lesson seemed to go on forever, and he was glad when it was finally time to unsaddle Red Fire.

He helped Hallie rub the horse down to speed up the process, then loaded him into the trailer. Evelyn drove them back to Caitlin's, making small talk all the way. He thanked her, as did Hallie, then unloaded the gelding and handed the lead rope to his daughter. "Go ahead and take him on home, honey. I'll be there in a minute."

"Okay."

He waited until Evelyn had also left, then turned to Caitlin. "Now do you want to tell me what's going on?"

"I already did."

"Caitlin, I know you mean well but—"

"That's right. You know I care about Hallie."

"I sure thought so."

"I do. What possible reason could I have to lie?"

"I don't know. I'm sure you're not doing it to be malicious, but Hallie's been through enough. Don't go putting nutty ideas into her head."

"Nutty?"

"Promise me you won't say anything to her, or I'll have to put a stop to the riding lessons and you can take Red Fire back."

"That would break Hallie's heart."

"Yes, it would. But you can't set her back when she's finally doing so well. I trust you'll keep quiet?"

She stared at him. "If I'd wanted to say anything to her, I wouldn't have made a point of talking to you. But I think you're making a mistake."

"Think what you want."

He saw anger and disbelief in her eyes. And sadness. "Goodbye, Alex." She stalked off.

Alex headed for home. Maybe Caitlin had a secret desire to be a mother and found Hallie a convenient surrogate child. Or maybe she was just so overwhelmed by what had happened with her own life, she needed something to focus on. A pet project. As soon as the uncharitable thought was out, he regretted it. Caitlin cared about Hallie.

But he still didn't trust anyone when it came to his daughter's well-being. Whatever Caitlin's motives or intentions, albeit good ones, her suggestion was ridiculous.

Bulimia.

Bullshit.

He found Hallie inside the barn, putting Red Fire in his stall for the night. Splash stood in the next stall. "So, did you have fun today?" he asked, scooping up an armful of hay.

"Yeah. Evelyn's nice. She's a really good rider." She tossed hay to Red Fire. "Dad, are you ticked off at Caitlin?"

"Why do you ask?"

"You didn't hardly talk to her on the way home."

Should he lie? He didn't want to tell his daughter what had happened. "I guess I'm just tired. I was up late last night working."

"On another kids' game." She looked at him accusingly. "I wish you'd finish Night Stalker."

"Hallie, you know why I won't."

She scooped grain, her expression unreadable. "I think it's stupid."

"What?"

"That you quit doing the really exciting games because of Melissa."

Momentarily at a loss for words, Alex could only stare at her. "Why do you think that?"

"Because. It wasn't a game that made those boys shoot her. It was because they're stupid, loser jerks." She blinked back angry tears. "Melissa liked your games."

"Well, I don't like them anymore and I'm not going to finish Night Stalker." He groped for a way to change the subject. "You're riding a lot better."

"Thanks." Hallie sulked a few more moments. "Evelyn was telling me that there's a big horse show coming up in Aspen with some of the top jumpers. She thought I might like to see it."

"Are you feeling up to it?"

"Yeah. Why?"

"Just making sure you don't still have the flu."

"I'm fine. So, can we go?"

"Sure."

"I want to ask Caitlin to come along with us, but I don't know if seeing the show would upset her."

"Could be." At the moment, he didn't want Caitlin anywhere near Hallie, but he knew that wasn't reasonable. She was right. Keeping the two of them apart would only hurt his daughter. "I guess you won't know unless you ask her."

"Maybe I will." She gave Red Fire a final pat, then

closed the stall door. "I'm hungry. What's for supper?"

"My special burritos."

She grinned at him. "I could eat a dozen."

He grinned back. "So could I. Wanna help me make them?"

"Sure."

They walked toward the house, Caitlin's accusations still floating in his mind. He'd keep an eye on Hallie. And if she continued to feel sick, he'd simply take her to see a doctor.

That would put an end to all speculation.

CHAPTER TWELVE

CAITLIN COULDN'T SLEEP. Alex's pigheadedness over Hallie had her tossing and turning until she finally got up and fired up her laptop. If he wouldn't listen to her, maybe he'd look at proof in plain black and white. Two hours later, she had a stack of printed pages on bulimia, including information on treatment and places to seek help. She shut off the computer and crawled into bed.

The next day she decided her near-empty cupboards and fridge called for a trip to the grocery store. It felt good being able to drive again. The sun was out, but the temperature remained cold. Daydreaming, Caitlin parked and went inside.

She was browsing through the snack and breakfast food aisle when she spotted Hallie and Alex.

"Hi, Caitlin," Hallie said.

"Hey, there." She put a box of granola bars in her buggy, ignoring Alex. *No easy task.* He looked hot in his tight jeans and cowboy hat. He wore a Carhartt jacket over his Western shirt—every inch the cowboy—as though he'd just come in off the range.

"Getting stocked up for Thanksgiving?" he asked. The holiday was less than three weeks away.

"No. Just grabbing a few items." She refused to look at him, pretending grave interest in choosing a jar of wheat germ.

"Hey, Caitlin," Hallie said. "Did your mom tell you about the horse show in Aspen next weekend?"

The one at the Circle J Ranch. The one she and Shauna always rode in. "Yeah, I know about it. Why?"

"You wanna go? Dad's taking me."

Go? She wanted to ride in it so badly, she felt sick. "I don't know, Hallie. I'll have to see what's going on."

"Okay." Hallie reached for a box of Twinkies. "Can I get these, Dad?"

"Sure."

Caitlin eyed the box in Hallie's hand.

"Something wrong?" Alex asked.

"No. Not a thing." It wasn't her place to judge what he let his daughter eat. Besides, she was more worried about the possibility of Hallie having bulimia and Alex's denial than she was about some stupid cupcakes.

"I love Twinkies," Hallie said, putting them in the buggy.

Caitlin shuddered. "I can't handle them. Too sweet."

"You're into health food, aren't you?" Hallie grimaced.

"Hey, it's not a crime." Caitlin bumped Hallie with her shoulder. "It's important to keep up a good diet for riding. That way you've got plenty of strength and stamina."

"Twinkies are dairy," Alex said. "They've got whipped cream."

Hallie laughed, and Alex grinned at her.

Caitlin wanted to smack him.

"Oh, crud," Hallie said. "I forgot my juice drinks. Be right back."

Caitlin faced Alex. "You won't think it's funny if your daughter ends up in the hospital."

"That's not going to happen." He stared defiantly at her.

She barely held her temper. "Alex, it's not a matter of Twinkies versus broccoli. I've got some stuff I printed off the Internet I'd like you to look at."

"What stuff?"

"Information on bulimia."

"I told you. My daughter does *not* have an eating disorder. Now do what I said and mind your own business." He gave his shopping cart a harder push than necessary, heading in the direction Hallie had gone.

Caitlin stood there, completely frustrated. She normally didn't butt into other people's business, but this was different. Hallie needed help, and she wasn't about to stand by and do nothing if the girl's own father was blind to that fact.

All the way home, she couldn't get Hallie off her mind. There had to be something she could do. As she was putting away her groceries, an idea came to mind. Caitlin picked up the phone and dialed Shauna's number.

"Hello?"

"Hey, girlfriend. What're you up to?"

"Just getting ready to go for a ride." Shauna was quiet for a split second. "Damn it, Caitlin, I'm sorry. I miss riding with you so much."

"It's okay. I'm not giving up yet." They'd had a good laugh over her escapade with Red Fire and the dog. "Are you riding in the Aspen show at the Circle J?"

"…Yes."

"Don't sound so guilty," Caitlin said. "I'm not going to fall apart just because my friend can still jump and I can't."

"But I feel awful entering without you. It won't be any fun to ride this year without you to compete against."

"Yeah, well, maybe you'll have a chance at winning then." They laughed. "Seriously, I was wondering if you knew if Kelly Walker is going to be there?"

"I imagine. She usually is."

"I know. But sometimes she goes to the show in Montrose instead."

"I can find out if you want. Any particular reason you're wondering?"

"I need a favor from her. I guess I can call her."

"Whatever you want."

"I'll see you in Aspen." They hung up, and Caitlin immediately looked up Kelly's number and dialed. No one answered, but she left a message, then put away the rest of her groceries.

Kelly had posed some serious competition a few years ago. Then she'd developed an eating disorder and had to check herself into a clinic. She'd suffered from anorexia, not bulimia. Still, having firsthand experience with an eating disorder... She might be able to help Hallie.

It was definitely worth a try. Caitlin didn't give a damn if Alex liked it or not.

IRONICALLY ALEX ended up getting the flu two days before the horse show. Caitlin hoped it would keep him home, so she'd be able to offer to take Hallie to the show herself, but no such luck. She'd already discussed matters with Kelly, who'd readily agreed to talk to Hallie. The best Caitlin could hope for was to find a way to introduce Hallie to Kelly when Alex wasn't right there watching—maybe when he went to the men's room or something.

They drove to the show in Alex's pickup—an uncomfortably tight fit on the small bench seat. Caitlin had thought of offering her Chevy for the trip, but then he'd probably think she was "butting in." At the indoor arena, she sat between him and Hallie in the bleachers. They'd come early to be sure to get good seats.

"Wow," Hallie said, staring in awe at the variety of jumps set up below them. "I can't wait for it to start."

"Would you like a tour of the show barn first?" Caitlin offered. It might be a great way to find Kelly. Why hadn't she thought of that sooner?

"You bet." Hallie rose to her feet.

"Can you hold our seats?" Caitlin asked Alex.

"Yeah, sure." His attitude toward her remained chilly.

Ignoring him, she laid her hand on Hallie's shoulder. "Come on, then. I'll introduce you around."

The familiar sights, sounds and scents of the show barn overwhelmed her once they were there. It was all she could do to stay cheerful as she led Hallie through the rows of stalls, keeping a watchful eye out for Kelly. She spotted her leading her bay from his stall.

"Hallie, I want you to meet a friend of mine," Caitlin said. "Come on."

"Caitlin," Kelly greeted her with a smile. "It's good to see you."

"You, too. I'd like you to meet my neighbor—Hallie Hunter. Hallie, Kelly Walker."

"Hi," Hallie said, stroking the bay's neck. "Your horse is gorgeous."

"Thank you. Caitlin tells me you've been riding Red Fire."

"That's right. I'm going to learn to do gymkhana."

"Fun." Kelly exchanged a glance with Caitlin. Where to begin?

"How long have you been jumping?" Hallie asked.

"Since I was in grade school."

"Have you been to the Olympics?"

"No, I'm afraid that's Caitlin's area of expertise. As a matter of fact, she generally kicks my butt in competition."

"Not anymore," Caitlin said.

"No, but you can't give up."

"I won't. You didn't." She gave Kelly a subtle nod.

"No, I didn't. When I was closest to dying, I think wanting to ride again was the only thing that gave me the courage to stick with my treatment program."

"What treatment program?" Hallie asked. "Were you on drugs?"

"No. I have an eating disorder. Anorexia."

Hallie looked sharply at her. "You don't look anorexic."

"That's because I've got it under control. At least I hope so. Hallie, Caitlin asked me to talk to you today, because she's worried about you."

"Why?" Hallie glared accusingly at Caitlin. "I don't have anorexia."

"No, but I think you have bulimia," Caitlin said softly. "You've been binging and purging, haven't you?"

"No!"

"Hallie—"

"I had the flu! God, why are you embarrassing me this way?"

"There's nothing to be embarrassed about," Kelly said. "Hallie, an eating disorder isn't something you can ignore or handle on your own. If you are binging and purging, you need to talk to your dad. Get some help. Believe me, I was just as hell-bent on denying my problem as you are. If it hadn't been for my family, I would've died."

"I'm not dying," Hallie said. "Just leave me the hell alone!" She all but ran from the show barn.

Caitlin raked her hand through her hair. "That went well."

"I'm sorry," Kelly said, genuinely upset. "I want to help her."

"So do I. You did your best."

"Keep me posted. And call if you want me to try again."

"Thanks." Caitlin hurried after Hallie. She found her sitting in the bleachers beside Alex. The girl refused to look at her. But she must've given her dad some plausible excuse as to why Caitlin hadn't returned right away, because he didn't seem suspicious or angry.

"Looks like they're getting ready to start." Alex indicated the group of riders lined up outside the arena gate.

"Yes." Caitlin took her seat. But her mind was on what had just happened. How could she get through to Hallie? She'd thought she'd found the perfect way—instead she'd blown it. She knew nothing about parenting. Now she was worried she'd done more harm than good. She supposed she'd have to tell Alex what happened. But she didn't want to do it here.

At an intermission between classes Hallie made a trip to the snack booth where she got an enormous soft pretzel with cheese and an extra-large Pepsi. She consumed them with relish, glancing defiantly at Caitlin. Alex didn't seem to notice.

Caitlin could barely concentrate on the horse show.

"YOU WANT TO TELL ME what's bothering you?" Alex sat across the dinner table from Hallie, picking at his spaghetti with a fork, his stomach still upset from his bout with the flu.

"Nothing."

"Come on, Hal. You've been sulking ever since we got home. What's the matter?"

"I told you—nothing." She stuffed a forkful of pasta into her mouth.

"Don't give me that. You were excited before the horse show, but you hardly talked on the way home." He studied her. "You didn't say a word to Caitlin. So all I can figure is something happened between the two of you while you were in the show barn. Want to tell me about it?"

"There's nothing to tell."

"Hallie." He laid his hand over hers, and made her look directly into his eyes.

"She introduced me to some friend of hers— Kelly. She has anorexia."

"What?"

"It was that girl on the big bay horse with the four white stockings. The one who took second place in the hunter class."

"I don't understand. How could she compete if she was anorexic?"

"She's been through treatment."

His anger began to build. "How do you know all this?"

"She told me. Caitlin and I talked to her in the barn."

"I see. What else did you talk about?"

Hallie lifted a shoulder and spoke around a mouthful of meatball. "Nothing really."

"So, why did finding out Caitlin's friend is anorexic upset you?"

She chewed and swallowed. "I don't know. I just didn't like hearing about it."

He checked the question he was about to ask. *Why would Caitlin do that?*

He knew the reason. And he was definitely going to have a talk with her.

After supper, Alex went straight to her house. Barely able to hold his temper in check, he pounded on the door with his fist. Spike started barking.

Caitlin opened the door, apprehension on her face. "Alex. You scared me. What's wrong?"

"I'll tell you what's wrong." He stormed across the threshold. "Your friend Kelly talking to my daughter."

She crossed her arms defensively. "I only want to help her."

He leaned close, resisting the temptation to shake her. "What part of 'butt out' don't you understand?"

"I won't butt out. Not when your daughter's life might be in danger." From the coffee table, she picked up a stack of papers and thrust them at him. "Here. Read these."

"I don't want them."

"You'd better want them, because Hallie needs help."

"You're not her mother!"

She shook the papers at him. "Read them."

"I'll bring your horse back tomorrow," he said, ignoring the out-thrust papers. "Hallie won't be taking riding lessons from you anymore."

Her arms dropped to her sides. "Alex, please don't do that. She's looking forward to riding in the gymkhana next month."

"I'll get her a horse of her own."

"But she won't be ready to ride in the gymkhana on a strange horse that quickly. She's comfortable with Red Fire. She can manage the novice events, but if you put her on a new horse..."

He glared at her. "You're using that as an excuse."

"I am not! I would never do anything to endanger Hallie. Why can't you get that through your thick head?"

"Me thick? You're the one who won't mind your own business." He stood there, torn. "All right. You can finish preparing her for the gymkhana, but that's it. And after it's over, you take Red Fire back. I'll finish teaching Hallie to ride. We're doing fine."

"Great. Good. You do that." She held the papers out again. "But will you at least read these? What can it hurt?"

He took the papers just to shut her up. "See you around."

"Get her help, Alex. Before it's too late."

He slammed the door shut behind him.

CHAPTER THIRTEEN

·

AFTER HER therapy session on Monday, Caitlin swam with Gran at the hot springs pool in Glenwood—something else her physical therapist recommended. All around them, snow fell in big, lazy flakes. Noreen sat, neck-deep in the water on the steps in the shallow end.

"How can I get through to him, Gran?" Caitlin asked. "I can't believe how bullheaded he is!"

"Honey, you can't. And I'm afraid that's all there is to it."

"But I have to keep trying—for Hallie's sake."

Gran pushed her silver hair back from her forehead. "He's right, you know. It is none of your business. Hallie's his child."

"Gran!"

"It's true. Doesn't mean he's right, but really, what *can* you do about it?"

"Make him see that he's wrong."

"How? You'll only make him angrier than he already is."

"I doubt that's possible."

Gran shrugged. "At least if you concede—apologize even—you can stay close to Hallie. Sounds like she needs you right now."

Apologize. Just the thought of it left her with a bad taste in her mouth. Alex was the one who should be apologizing—to Hallie. *The numbskull.*

"Come on, now." Gran gave her arm a pat. "Put it out of your mind for the moment. You're supposed to be enjoying this. Just look at that view." They were surrounded by snow-blanketed mountains. "I love it here," Gran said. "There aren't a lot of places you can swim in the snow."

"True." Caitlin floated on her back, trying to relax. But she couldn't get her mind off Alex and Hallie. An hour later she showered in the locker room, dressed and blow-dried her hair.

At home she bid Gran goodbye, let Spike out in the yard, then headed straight over to Alex's house. Now would be a good time to talk, while Hallie was at school. He opened the door with a scowl already on his face.

"Don't look so sour. I came to apologize."

He held the door open. "Come in."

Seated on his couch, Caitlin felt awkward. A far cry from the last time she'd been in here, having breakfast with him and Hallie. "Look, Alex. I'm not sorry I tried to help your daughter. But I do apologize for stepping on your toes. You're right. She's yours to raise as you see fit."

"I'm glad you finally realize that." His features softened. "I love my little girl. I would never let any harm come to her."

Then read the damned papers.

With effort, Caitlin held her tongue. Gran had a point. "I know. Can we talk about something else?"

"Sure. What do you want to talk about?"

"The gymkhana. I thought I'd bring barrels and poles over to set up some practice courses for her. The snow's nearly all melted." Glenwood Springs had gotten six inches on Friday to their two.

"Barrels?"

"She's not ready for barrel racing yet, of course. But she can do the flag race at a lope. We'll need barrels for that, and a couple of buckets. And she can do ring spearing. I don't have anything to practice that with, but it's fun, and she doesn't have to go fast. We'll use the poles to make a keyhole pattern. She can take that at her own pace, as well." She shrugged. "For that matter, she could lope the barrels. But I'm afraid Red Fire might get excited and take off with her. He knows the pattern so well."

"Will he do that in the other events?"

She shook her head. "I don't think so, but that's why I want to practice them—to make sure. I never ran flags or keyhole with him, so he shouldn't get too worked up. If we were preparing for serious competition, Hallie would have to practice for months. But this is just a Fun Day."

"Sounds good. I'm sure she'll be excited."

"Great." She hoped so. Hallie might still be angry with her. "Then I'll go over to Foxwood and get the stuff we'll be using."

"Need a hand?"

She started to refuse—the stable hands would load the barrels and poles for her—but the more she could put Alex at ease, the better chance she had of getting through to him. "Sure."

He grabbed his hat. "Let's go."

At Foxwood, they loaded two fifty-five-gallon barrels, two plastic five-gallon buckets and four PVC poles on stands. "The flags," Caitlin said, snapping her fingers. She returned to the tack room. Once she had them, she double-checked to make sure that was everything they would need. "That should do it. If the weather turns on us again, we can bring Hallie over here to Foxwood. We've got more barrels and poles we can use, so we don't have to haul the stuff back and forth."

"All right."

They climbed in the truck and headed homeward. "So, what are you and Hallie doing for Thanksgiving?"

"I don't know. I'll probably take her out someplace."

"Out?" Caitlin waved her hand. "You don't want to eat at a restaurant on Thanksgiving. Why don't the two of you come to Foxwood?"

"I don't want to intrude on a family holiday."

"You won't be intruding. Our chef makes enough food for the army anyway, so there'll be plenty."

"Your chef?" He raised his eyebrows.

She glanced over at him and laughed. "Yeah. Didn't I mention that no one in our family cooks very well?"

He grinned. "I've never been served by a personal chef before. Hallie would get a real kick out of that." Then he sobered. "You're not doing this to prove something to me, are you?"

"What do you mean?"

"You know. About Hallie and what all she eats."

"No." She tried not to let her disappointment in him show. "My only motive is being neighborly."

"All right. In that case, I accept."

"Good." She dropped him off at his house. "I'll be back as soon as Hallie gets home from school so she can help set this stuff up. It'll be fun."

"Will do." He gave her the thumbs-up, and Caitlin drove across the road.

She really hadn't meant anything by inviting him and Hallie for the holiday. But when he brought it up, she realized it might be an idea. Everyone over-ate at Thanksgiving, especially on home-cooked food. But generally, people slept off their meal rather than throwing it back up.

Surely if Hallie did that, he couldn't write off her illness this time.

Not if he had half a brain.

HALLIE TROTTED Red Fire around the outside of one of two barrels set opposite each other at the end of the arena. With a neon orange flag tied to a wooden stake gripped in her right hand, she slowed the horse to a walk at Caitlin's instruction, plopped the flag into the oat-filled, five-gallon bucket, moved on to the second barrel, retrieved the flag protruding from that bucket and headed back to the finish line.

"Good job," Caitlin called.

"This is fun!" Hallie's eyes shone as she pulled the gelding to a halt.

"I'll move the flag and you can go again."

"I'll get it," Alex said. He hustled down to the opposite end of the arena and switched the flag back over to the right barrel.

Caitlin resented the fact that she could no longer jog the length of the arena with such ease. But she focused on Hallie. After practicing a few runs at the flag race, they set the four poles in a rectangular pattern and Caitlin instructed Hallie on the keyhole event. "Ride your horse between the poles—just past them—spin around and ride back out." It was normally a fast-paced event, over in a few seconds. But Hallie took it at a trot.

"I'm going too slow," she complained upon returning.

"No, you're not," Caitlin said, laying her hand on Red Fire's neck. "You're not ready to run yet, kiddo. Be patient. By next summer, you'll be burning up the barrels, poles…everything."

"Next summer," Hallie harrumphed. "That's forever."

Caitlin and Alex both laughed. "It'll go before you know it, Hal," Alex said.

The sun began to sink low in the sky, and with it, the temperature dropped drastically. "I think we'd better hold off on the ring spearing until tomorrow," Caitlin said. "I'm getting cold."

"Not me," Hallie said with a grin. She leaned down and hugged Red Fire's neck with both arms. "I'm warm and cozy on this fuzzy horse."

"Yeah, well I'm freezing my tush off in this ice-cold arena." Caitlin shot her a teasing smile. "So I'm out of here. You can let your old man help you brush your horse down."

"Old man?" Alex made a face at her.

"You mean *your* horse," Hallie said.

"Well, he's sort of yours." Caitlin patted Red Fire's neck. She hoped Alex had changed his mind about sending the chestnut back after the gymkhana.

Surely he had, now that he'd cooled down and accepted her apology.

"Thanks, Caitlin," he said.

"Yeah, thanks," Hallie added. "I had fun."

"I'm glad, and you're more than welcome."

"See you later," Alex said.

HE WENT OVER to her house the next morning, shortly before lunchtime. He wanted to talk to her while Hallie wasn't around. Spike ran down the driveway, barking, then headed toward the barn. Alex followed him, knowing Caitlin wouldn't leave the dog running loose if she weren't with him. Sure enough, she had Silver Fox in cross ties, and was grooming the enormous horse. She wore a T-shirt beneath an unbuttoned flannel shirt, her jacket unzipped.

"Going for another ride?" Alex asked.

"No. I don't think I'm up for one yet. But Fox needed a good brushing."

"Want some help?"

"Sure, if you'd like."

He picked up a mane-and-tail comb from the purple tote tray she'd set in the aisle, and went to work on the gray's long tail.

"You might want to put some conditioner on his tail before you try to comb it out," Caitlin said. "Otherwise, it tends to break the hair."

"Right." He searched the tray, found a leave-in

equine conditioner, and poured some into the palm of his hand. It was a nasty yellow-green, but it smelled okay. "This enough?"

"For one section." She smiled at him, and he nearly forgot he'd been mad at her. "So, what are you up to this morning?"

"Actually, I wanted to talk to you about something."

"Oh?"

"Hallie's birthday is coming up. She told me she wants you to be there for it. We're going out to dinner."

"She mentioned that."

"So, you'll come?"

"Sure." She paused in her task of brushing Silver Fox's back. "You walked over here instead of calling to ask me that?"

"No. I came to tell you I'm sorry I was so hard on you." He shifted, uncomfortable. He hated to admit being wrong when he really didn't think he was. "I know you meant well. I shouldn't have come down on you like that. I'm a little overprotective when it comes to Hallie."

"Really? I hadn't noticed."

"I just want to make one thing clear. You and I will get along fine if you keep your opinions on my daughter to yourself."

"I already got that, Alex." She pursed her lips in

a straight line. "You don't have to print it on a T-shirt for me."

"I'm not just talking about voicing them to me," he said. "I don't want you telling other people things concerning our private business. And I sure as hell don't want you saying anything more to Hallie. Understood?"

"Yes." Her jaw set, she continued brushing Silver Fox, avoiding eye contact with him.

"Good. Then let's forget about it." They worked in silence. Alex's hands grew cramped and tired, combing the tangles out of Fox's long, thick tail. "Lordy, how in the world do you manage to groom him regularly? Or is that what stable hands are for?"

"Sometimes. But I prefer to take care of my own horses. The hired hands pick up the slack." She patted the gray's neck. "I'm thinking about bringing Black Knight over here, too. I miss him, and Fox could use the company now that Red Fire's at your place."

"Might be a good idea." He stepped up beside her, and went to work on the gelding's mane. They were silent again, lost in their work. Caitlin moved from the near side of Fox, coming around to the off side where Alex stood. As she worked a stiff-bristled brush over the gelding's coat, she unconsciously moved closer to Alex. They bumped shoulders, glanced up and smiled at each other.

"Sorry," she said. "My fault."

"No problem." Before he could stop himself, he caressed her cheek with the back of his hand. "Your skin's soft."

"Where is that coming from?" She stepped away, out of reach.

"I was remembering the day of the blizzard."

"Oh." She chewed her bottom lip. "I thought we agreed that was a mistake."

"You thought it was. Me, I liked it."

"I…"

"What? You liked it, too?" He knew she had. Why she'd suddenly pulled away and told him she didn't want to get involved, he still couldn't figure.

"No. Yes. I mean, that's not what I was going to say." He waited. "I was trying to think of a way to tell you I hadn't meant to be so abrupt. I have my reasons, that's all."

"Really." He stepped closer. With one finger he tilted her chin up. "What reasons are those, Caitlin?"

"Nothing you need to know about. I just…" She licked her lips.

No matter what she said, he knew she wanted to kiss him. He could see it in her eyes. Slowly, giving her plenty of time to pull back, he leaned over and brushed his lips against hers. She moaned softly, closing her eyes, parting her lips. Dropping the comb to the floor, he slid his arms around her waist, kissing her gently, then taking her mouth eagerly as she responded. She sank into him, letting go of the brush she'd held, and looped her arms around his neck.

They kissed like two people who hadn't known this kind of pleasure in a long time. Like lovers denied. He'd felt denied all right, from the day when she'd pushed him away. Damned if he could figure out what it was about her that drew him to her even when he was angry with her. He wondered if they'd be the sort of couple who would fight, then make up between the sheets. The idea stirred his flesh, and he tucked Caitlin's hips against his.

"Alex, we can't."

"Why not?" he murmured against her lips. "We're both of age."

"It's not that. Oh, damn." She clenched her hands against his shoulders, then kissed him again. Over and over. "No. Wait. Stop."

Frustrated, he pulled back. "Caitlin, what's the matter?"

It took her half a minute to answer. "Me," she finally said. "It's me, Alex."

"What do you mean?"

"Look at me." She swept her hands over the length of her body.

"I'm looking. And I like what I see."

"No, I mean really look." She held out her arms.

"I limp when I walk, my hip is all messed up, and my back…"

"Come with me," he said.

"What?"

Ignoring her protests, he took her by the hand and led her to the house. He marched her straight over to the mirror in her dining room. "Look in there," he commanded. "Go on."

She sighed. "Your point is?"

"Do you see anything wrong with your reflection?"

"I've never liked my nose, and my chin is too square."

"That's a matter of opinion. But that's not what I mean. Look closely."

"My face didn't get messed up in the crash. Just my head."

"Well, apparently the crash caused brain damage if you think there's anything wrong with your body. Do you have a bigger mirror?"

"What for?" But she looked at him as though already guessing the answer.

"Where is it? Must be in your bedroom, because I didn't see it in your bathroom. Come on."

He marched her down the hall. "The other way," she said, as he stopped in front of an empty bedroom.

He spun her by the shoulders and walked up to the full-length mirror mounted to the back of her closet door. "Now, take a good, hard look," he said. "There's not a damned thing wrong with your body, either. Not to me."

"That's because you haven't seen me without my clothes." She winced. "That didn't come out right, but you know what I meant."

"We can remedy that," he said, slipping his arms around her from behind, watching her reflection.

"Definitely not." She shrugged out of his grasp.

"Why?"

"Because." She lowered her gaze. "You wouldn't like what you see."

"Let me be the judge of that." He took hold of her jacket and slipped it off her shoulders.

"Are you propositioning me?"

"That's not a very nice way to put it," he said. He slid his arms around her again. "I'd rather seduce you."

"Alex."

"What?"

"We left Silver Fox tied in the barn."

"He'll be all right." He leaned one palm against the wall. "Come on, at least take off your shirt."

"You've got a lot of nerve."

He laughed. "Just the flannel."

She looked exasperated, but slipped out of the long-sleeved shirt.

"Now turn around," he said, pointing her at the mirror again. "Take a look. What do you see?"

"A woman who's going to freeze when she goes back out to tend to her horse."

"Come on, Caitlin. Let's be serious for a minute."

"I am being serious." She looked him straight in the eye. "Making me look at myself in a mirror isn't going to change what I feel. But maybe I can change what you think you're feeling." She jerked her T-shirt out from the waistband of her jeans. "You want to see for yourself? I'll show you."

Before he could open his mouth, she'd yanked the T-shirt over her head. Beneath it, she wore a lacy pink bra that barely concealed her nipples. His blood pulsed. He hadn't meant for things to go this far. Of course, if she was headed where he hoped, he'd be more than willing.

She didn't stop with the T-shirt. She undid her jeans and stepped out of them, as well. "There," she said, holding her arms out. "Now, *you* tell me what *you* see."

A woman I want to make love to.

"A crazy woman in pink underwear and socks."

"Alex."

"What do you want me to say? That there's something wrong with you?"

"There is."

"Not hardly. All I see is that small scar on the inside of your knee. And a little one right there." He brushed his fingers over her shoulder, to a jagged white line below her collarbone.

"Small and little are hardly accurate." She stared at him. "Then there's the way my body's shaped and the way I move—or should I say the way I no longer move."

"There's nothing wrong with your figure, or the way you move."

"I'm not talking about my curves," Caitlin said. "My arm still curls, and my hip feels like it's about to pop out of the socket all the time. Makes me walk funny."

"It just gives a sexy little bump to your walk."

"A sexy bump? Right. My back is messed up. My head." She gestured. "I can't balance right, can't control my body. I can't ride, so I doubt I'd be able to…do anything else without major pain."

He took hold of her and made her face her reflection once more. "You're beautiful, inside and out." Moving her hair out of the way, he kissed her neck, then moved his lips to trace her scars. "I want to try to make you feel good without hurting you."

"Even if that's possible, I probably can't move enough to…be any fun." Color rose to her cheeks.

"Why don't you let me be the judge of that?" He'd told himself he'd never trust a woman again. But he'd known this moment was coming ever since he'd first laid eyes on Caitlin.

She met his gaze in the mirror. "Do you really think I'm attractive?"

"If you can't see what I see in that mirror, then I don't know what else to tell you." With effort, he stepped away from her.

Caitlin spun around and grabbed him by the belt. "Not so fast." She pulled him close. "I know what to tell you."

"What's that?"

"I want you. Badly."

"Is that so?"

"Yeah, it is. Come here." She tugged on his belt, and he leaned into her.

"As long as you're asking." He pulled her against him, taking her mouth with his.

CHAPTER FOURTEEN

CAITLIN KNEW she'd taken leave of her senses, but she didn't care. She kissed Alex hard, her body aching for a man's touch. But not just any man's. She'd tried to keep an emotional distance from him, but there was no denying what she felt. He made her madder than hell at times, but she truly cared about him. More than that, she could let herself love him if she wasn't careful. So she blocked out her thoughts and lost herself in the wonderful touch of his hands and mouth on her body.

He lifted her carefully and placed her on the bed. "Are your feet cold, or can I take off your socks?" He grinned crookedly.

"My feet aren't cold, and I don't have cold feet." Not anymore, after what he'd said to her. No other man had ever expressed his feelings to her so eloquently. "You can take off anything you want to."

"I like a woman who doesn't mince words." He pulled her socks off, then yanked off his shirt and stretched out on the bed beside her. Cradling her in his arms, he kissed her neck, giving her shivers, working his way across her shoulder. His hand reached to unsnap her bra. It took him a couple of tries, and somehow she was glad he wasn't one of those smooth movers who snapped your bra off with the flick of finger and thumb. That probably meant he didn't do this all the time. That he wasn't coming on to her just to satisfy his needs.

Stop thinking!

She moaned as his hands found her breasts. He'd slipped her bra off, and he cupped her, fondling, kissing her. Taking her into his mouth to suck gently. He used his tongue to lave one nipple, then the other, and the sensation made her arch her back and suck in her breath. She kneaded the muscles of his shoulders, his biceps. Lord, he felt so hard, so good.

She felt wanton, lying near-naked beside him in a bed that was normally empty and lonely. She shivered.

"Cold?" He pulled back the covers, and Caitlin slipped beneath them.

She undid the button on his jeans, then slid the zipper down, enjoying the anticipation. He stood and yanked his jeans off, revealing a pair of practical, dark blue boxers. But somehow they looked every bit as sexy on him as a tight pair of briefs. Maybe even more so. They still couldn't hide his desire for her. Caitlin skimmed her fingers over his hardness and he groaned, closing his eyes. "God, you're making me crazy."

"Good." She gave him an impish smile, then slid his boxers down. Her hip twinged as she leaned forward to take him in her mouth, but she was beyond caring. Moisture gathered between her legs, along with a sweet ache as she let her tongue caress and tease. She held him, touching, rubbing, making him draw in his breath and moan as he grew harder.

"If you don't stop that, it'll be all over," he groaned, pressing her gently back onto the covers. "My turn." He slid her panties down, and then kissed her from her lips to her breasts, and down to her stomach. He paused near her belly button, licking and teasing her. Making her arch her hips with longing.

"Please, Alex," she gasped. "I need you."

"Slow down, sweetness," he said. "I'm going to make this good for you."

"It's already good." She tried to pull him on top of her, but he would have none of it. He used his mouth and his tongue in ways she'd never thought possible, making her so wild, she thought her brain might explode. With a sharp cry, she rocked against his mouth, arching her hips, shoving her hands through his hair. Her body shuddered and contracted, and she peaked in wave after wave of pleasure.

Then Alex was inside her, and she could feel the thin latex between them. She looked down at their joined bodies and moaned. He was gorgeous. A perfectly formed male, and she loved looking at him. His chest was hard and still bore the lingering bronze of a suntan. A thin mat of dark hair sprinkled across it, and Caitlin raised her mouth to kiss his chest, to lick his nipples. He slid his hands lower on her back, grasping the arch of it with one hand. With the other, he pressed her buttocks to him, bringing their bodies tightly together. He rocked with a gentle rhythm that became more frantic as he moved inside her.

Caitlin felt her desire building again. A tension she both wanted to prolong and to release. "Alex." His name was a sob on her lips as she came again, clutching her legs around his waist without thought. Holding him tightly against her. She arched upward in a way she'd never thought herself capable of moving again.

He let out a deep cry, then nipped her shoulder. His hips thrust hard, again and again as the pleasure rocked through him, into her. Making hers intensify. She nipped him back at his neck, then hungrily sought his lips, needing the completion of tasting him again. Of having his tongue inside her mouth. He kissed her long and hard. Then more softly, until finally he collapsed with his head on her shoulder, breathing fast. Their skin was moist and warm, and

Caitlin loved the way he felt. Loved his weight on her body. It took a long minute for her to feel the pain that had come as a price.

Her hip began to throb, her knee ached. And her back felt plain numb. But she didn't care. She'd gladly do it all over again. Right now.

Alex raised up on the palms of his hands. "Am I hurting you?"

"No," she lied. She squeezed his buttocks. "Stay where you are. Mmm." She closed her eyes, running her hands over his back. He groaned with pleasure and lay still, nibbling her earlobe.

"I told you," he said. "You're beautiful inside and out. You made me feel so good."

"Mmm, ditto, cowboy." She wished they could stay like this forever. She loved the warmth of his body. Loved sharing her bed with him, and wished he could spend the night. "I've heard of nooners, but I never had one before."

"Is that right?" He opened his eyes to look directly at her.

"That's right. As a matter of fact, I've only had one serious boyfriend."

He grinned. "What happened to him?"

"We both thought more of riding the show circuit than of each other. Things just sort of drifted apart. I went to CSU, he went on to UCLA."

"I'm glad."

"That he went to UCLA?" She pressed her lips together, holding back the smile.

"That he's not in your life anymore."

"What about you?" She couldn't help asking, but wasn't sure she really wanted to know the answer. Surely he'd had dozens of women.

"No, I never went to UCLA."

She smacked him lightly. "Stop it."

He sobered. "There was Hallie's mother, and a few women here and there who meant very little to me." He brushed the hair off her forehead. "I care about you, Caitlin. I like where we just went. I wasn't expecting it yet, but I'm glad it happened."

"Me, too."

He kissed her. "Would you feel up to a repeat performance?"

She rolled over on top of him. "Bring it on."

AFTER ALEX LEFT, Caitlin languished in bed. He'd promised to turn Silver Fox out in the pasture, and told her there was no sense in both of them getting cold. Part of her had wanted to go outside with him. But another part wanted to lie there and soak up the scents of their lovemaking…the coziness of the bedsheets, still warm from his body. Caitlin dozed, and when she woke up, it was after three o'clock.

Nothing like sex to make you sleep like a rock.

She took a shower, then let Spike out in the yard.

Alex had apparently let him in when he'd left. She'd been so engrossed in what was happening between them, she'd forgotten the little terrier was outside. "I'm surprised you didn't run off," she said, stepping out the door with him. The air felt crisp and fresh. Wonderful. She couldn't remember when she'd felt better.

But when Caitlin looked across the street, reality began to creep in, spoiling her mood. Hallie would be home from school soon. Thinking of her brought to mind Caitlin's last argument with Alex. She'd probably made a mistake in sleeping with him.

She didn't want it to be a mistake. She wanted it to be as right as the memory of their lovemaking. Wanted things between her and Alex to grow. Maybe they would.

One day at a time.

ON THE NIGHT of Hallie's birthday, Alex picked Caitlin up at six-thirty. He'd made reservations at Bella Luna for 7:00 p.m.

She climbed into the Ranger beside Hallie. "Happy birthday, kiddo." Smiling, Caitlin handed her a gift-wrapped box.

"Thanks." Hallie's face brightened. "Can I open it now?"

"If you can find elbow room." She laughed. "Alex, we can drive my truck if you want."

"Maybe we'd better." The Ranger was only big enough for him and Hallie. He'd never imagined the possibility that might change. Reminding himself that it actually hadn't, he took the keys Caitlin offered.

Hallie tore the wrapping from her gift as they headed down the road. "Oh, my God. Caitlin, thank you." Hallie held up a peach, silk Western shirt, with fancy stitching and a chestnut horse head embroidered on the yoke. "It looks like Red Fire."

"That's because it is. I bought the shirt and had the design done by a friend of Gran's. It's for you to wear at the gymkhana."

"Thank you, so much. This is adorable!" She grinned, and Alex knew that whatever had gone on between her and Caitlin, all was forgiven.

At Bella Luna, the hostess seated them at a table on the far side of the restaurant. Caitlin ordered steak and lobster, and to Alex's surprise, so did Hallie. "I didn't know you were into seafood, Hal."

She shrugged. "I thought I'd try it."

He couldn't help but wonder if it was yet another way in which Hallie strove to emulate Caitlin. He wasn't sure what she'd said to Hallie the other day when they'd been practicing in the arena, but it must've been enough to restore Caitlin's hero status in Hallie's eyes.

"So," Alex said, laying down his menu. "How are things going with your physical therapy?"

"Pretty well. As a matter of fact, I've been progressing enough that I've definitely decided to go back to school."

"School?" Hallie looked up sharply from the dessert menu she'd been browsing. "You're leaving?"

"For a little while. I just haven't decided when." Caitlin obviously didn't catch the distress in Hallie's eyes.

Alex could have kicked himself. This was exactly what he'd hoped to avoid—upsetting Hallie. "It's only for a semester, Hal," he said.

"Are you going back to CSU?" Hallie asked.

"Uh-huh."

"Good. I'm glad you're not moving to another state."

"Are you kidding?" Caitlin smiled. "I'd get homesick if I left Colorado."

"I like it here, too," Hallie said.

"Have you made a lot of friends at school?"

"Sort of." She gave her attention back to the dessert menu.

"It takes time," Caitlin said. "Don't worry, kiddo, you'll have plenty when you start gymkhana."

The restaurant was busy, and Alex drank two glasses of Pepsi waiting for their food to arrive. Halfway through the meal, his overindulgence caught up with him. "Excuse me. Gotta see a man about a horse."

He made his way to the men's room.

CAITLIN TOOK a bite of her baked potato, wondering what to say to Hallie. She'd apologized for upsetting her as they'd set up the arena obstacles the other day. Hallie had accepted it, and obviously wasn't mad at her anymore. But where did she go from here? There had to be a way to get Hallie to open up to Alex. Honesty with her father was the only way Caitlin could see for her to get the help she needed.

"Hi, Caitlin."

She looked up to see Kelly Walker approaching their table. "Kelly." *Talk about lousy timing.* "What are you doing here?"

"Having dinner." Kelly looked at her strangely. "Hi, Hallie, how are you?"

"Fine." Hallie didn't return Kelly's smile.

"We're here celebrating Hallie's thirteenth birthday," Caitlin said.

"Neat. A teenager now. Happy birthday, Hallie."

"Thanks."

"So, how've you been?"

"Well, I'm not going to puke up my birthday cake, if that's what you're getting at."

Kelly's face went crimson.

Caitlin sucked in her breath.

And looked up to see Alex, standing near the booth, just behind Hallie's elbow.

"What's going on?" he asked, his expression every bit as grave as his daughter's.

Hallie started guiltily, then went back to picking at her lobster.

"Nothing," Caitlin said, her eyes begging him not to cause a scene. "Kelly was just leaving."

"Yeah, see you later, Caitlin. Have a fun birthday, Hallie."

Alex slid into the booth next to his daughter. Caitlin waited for him to say something about Hallie's comment, but he didn't. The silence seemed to go on forever.

"Six more days 'til Thanksgiving," she finally said. "Hey, Hallie, have you ever been on a sleigh ride?"

"No."

"It's a family tradition at Foxwood Farms to go on a sleigh ride Thanksgiving Day. You know—over the river and all that. Of course, we don't always get snow, in which case, we substitute a hayride." She smiled. Hallie didn't, but she looked interested.

"Really?"

"Uh-huh. You want to come?"

"I guess."

"How about you?" she asked Alex.

"Sounds fun."

"Good. Then plan to come early. We usually take off about 10:00 a.m. That way we've got plenty of time to enjoy ourselves before dinner."

They finished their meal. Alex paid, then walked beside Caitlin to the parking lot. "You'd better have a talk with your friend," he said, quietly enough that Hailie couldn't hear.

"Aren't you even the least bit curious why your daughter made that comment?"

"I already know why," he said. "She told me Kelly upset her, talking about her anorexia. Apparently Hailie doesn't appreciate Kelly's insinuations any more than I do. Let's make sure she stays away from my daughter."

He strode ahead to unlock the truck.

Caitlin could barely hold her tongue.

She marched to the truck, more determined than ever to get through to Hailie and make her come clean to Alex.

MOTHER NATURE hinted at snow the day before the holiday, but there was only a light dusting on the ground by Thanksgiving morning. Hardly enough for a sleigh ride.

"Where's that blizzard when we need it?" Benton Kramer looked up at the gray sky as he and Dillon hitched two Belgians to a wagon.

"I didn't know you had a team," Alex said. "How'd I miss them when you gave us the tour, Caitlin?"

"Dad bartered for them. It's another tradition. Every year he borrows his golf partner's team in exchange for one of our sleighs on Christmas Eve if it snows."

"And if it doesn't?"

"Then Harry gives a neighborhood hayride, and Dad owes him big-time." She laughed.

"You and your bartering," Evelyn said, kissing her husband's cheek. "I think you just enjoy dickering with Harry, no matter what it's over."

Caitlin watched her parents. She'd always taken the love they shared for granted. Had thought everyone's parents were that way. Until she'd gotten old enough to realize. She'd never thought much about what she wanted in a man if she were to marry, since marriage had never been a part of her plans. But now, as she looked at Alex—sexy in his black hat, boots and a sheepskin-lined jacket—her mind began to play not "what if," but "what would."

What would it be like to share her life with Alex? To be more than Hallie's mentor?

A short time later, she piled into the straw-filled wagon with her aunts and uncles, cousins, plus her parents, Gran and Dillon. Hallie and Alex felt like an extension of that family as Caitlin sank beside them on a straw bale. Her father took the reins, her mother beside him on the wagon seat. Everyone else burrowed beneath heavy wool blankets, sitting on rows of straw. With the temperature a chilly twenty-seven degrees, it didn't take long for noses to turn red and cheeks to glow.

"Man, I'll be looking forward to some hot chocolate when we get back," Dillon said. "Or maybe a hot toddy."

"What's that?" Hallie asked.

"Nothing you need to worry about," Alex said.

"I get it. It's alcohol."

"Hey, I only drink on special occasions," Dillon replied. "Speaking of which, I hear you're helping Shauna out with the gymkhana next weekend."

"Yep." Caitlin burrowed deeper beneath the blanket, hunching her shoulders against the cold. And felt Alex's arm slip around her. The unexpected gesture startled her so that she nearly lost her train of thought. "I—uh—thought it might be fun. There'll be Western and English pleasure events on Saturday, and speed events Sunday. Can you believe they're actually calling it 'Sunday Fun Day'?"

Dillon laughed. "Hey, it rhymes."

"I can't wait," Hallie said. She cuddled Spike in her lap. "But I'm glad the arena is indoors. Man, it is cold!"

"Want to help in the kitchen when we get back?" Caitlin asked. "That'll warm you up."

"I thought you had a chef."

"We do. But I still like to get my hands into something. Usually I make a fruit salad or a veggie platter. Nothing fancy."

"Yeah, and believe me, you don't want to warm up with her version of hot chocolate," Alex said.

"Skim-milk, sugar-free, diet crapola." He gave her a squeeze.

"Hey, don't make fun of my hot chocolate. Besides, Mom serves the real deal on holidays."

She wasn't entirely sure she felt comfortable sitting this way, so close to him, with Hallie around. But then, Hallie was no dummy. Surely she sensed something more than friendship between her and Alex.

The real deal.

Was that what she had with him? Caitlin had no way of telling, nothing to compare it to. All she knew was she'd enjoyed making love with him. So much so, she'd let him right back into her bed on two other occasions since. Having Hallie at school and Alex working out of his house gave them plenty of time alone. She kept telling herself to relax and enjoy what was happening between them. To take things one day at a time.

If things were going anywhere for them, she felt even more of an obligation to look out for Hallie's best interests.

"Wow, THIS KITCHEN is huge." Hallie eyed the room with its two restaurant-size stoves, enormous stainless steel refrigerator and spacious island with shiny cookware hung above.

The chef gave her a wink, smiling as he and his staff hustled to prepare the food.

"Yeah, too bad I'm not a better cook so I could

enjoy it more." Caitlin pulled items from the cupboards and refrigerator and began to prepare a fruit salad. She gave Hallie some kiwi to cut and put in a bowl. They added deep purple grapes and a handful of sliced almonds.

"Wow, that looks pretty good," Hallie said.

Caitlin handed her a spoon. "Taste it."

"Mmm. Not bad."

"See? Healthy food can be fun."

Hallie gave her a dull look. "I know."

Caitlin stirred the salad. "Hallie, you're a good-looking young woman—and a smart one. There's no reason to let your peers pressure you into thinking otherwise."

"I don't."

"Good." She topped the salad with a sprig of fresh mint. "There's also no reason why you can't open up to your dad. He loves you. That's why he's so darned overprotective."

"I know."

She touched Hallie's wrist. "Talk to him, honey. Not for me. For you."

CHAPTER FIFTEEN

ALEX SLID a bite of honey-cured ham, sliced paper-thin, into his mouth. It practically melted on his tongue. He'd seen some pretty good Thanksgiving spreads in his time, but none like this one. In addition to the traditional dishes like ham, turkey, cranberries and sweet potatoes, the Kramers' chef had concocted a variety of exotic temptations. Alex wasn't even sure what some of them were, but they all looked and smelled good.

He'd kept a close eye on Hallie throughout the day, watching for any sign that she didn't feel well. But she seemed fine, eating with the same enthusiasm as everyone else. Alex was on his second helping, absorbed in conversation with Benton, when he heard Hallie ask Noreen where the restroom was. He caught Caitlin's eye, but she quickly glanced down at her plate.

Hallie needed to use the bathroom. So what?

He kept listening to Benton's story about a hunter jumper he'd owned and showed a few years ago. But his mind was on Hallie. He didn't want to believe Caitlin's suspicions. But he had to make sure nothing was wrong with his daughter.

Several minutes later, Hallie had yet to return to the table. Alex waited for a break in the conversation, then excused himself. He'd heard Noreen tell Hallie where the nearest bathroom was, so he headed that way.

But the door stood ajar, the room empty. He continued down the hall. "Hallie?" The rooms along the way were either closed or unoccupied. He was about to start tapping on doors, looking for a second bathroom, when he came to the back staircase. And there was Hallie, tiptoeing down the carpeted steps.

"Hal, what are you doing?"

She clamped a hand to her chest. "Dad—you scared me."

"Why were you upstairs?"

She looked guilty. "Um—I wanted to see what it looked like."

"That's not polite. Why didn't you wait and ask Caitlin to show you around?"

"I dunno." She avoided direct eye contact. "I just wanted to see the upstairs. Jeez, Dad, it's no big deal. I'm sorry." She flounced past him.

He followed, relieved to see she seemed to be okay. No more flu. Nothing weird going on. Just a typical kid, being nosy, though snooping really wasn't typical of Hallie. He'd taught her better manners than that. Maybe wandering through the Kramers' house meant she'd grown comfortable enough with them, Caitlin in particular, to feel at home. It was a big step for her. Again, he thanked his lucky stars Caitlin had helped pull Hallie out of her shell, and vowed not to be so hard on her. She meant well. He'd simply have to make sure she knew the boundaries when it came to his daughter.

Hallie would miss Caitlin when she headed back to CSU. *Hell, who was he kidding? He'd miss her, too.*

Back in the dining room, Hallie had taken her seat and was working on finishing a buttered roll when the kitchen staff brought out an array of desserts. Hallie cut into a slice of pumpkin pie, heaped with whipped cream. But that didn't worry Alex. She'd eaten the fruit salad Caitlin had made, and all of her vegetables. Hallie was a growing kid with a healthy appetite.

Nothing more.

THE WEEK SPED BY, with Caitlin helping Shauna prepare for the gymkhana. It was set for the first weekend in December, and they'd worked hard organizing the event. Hallie had helped hang flyers around town, anxious for the weekend to get there. Only one small hitch had come up in their plans.

With Dillon out of town, and Caitlin's mom and

dad away at a horse show in Arizona, there was no one to haul Red Fire to the indoor arena in Ferguson. Shauna had enough on her hands overseeing the horse show on Saturday and the gymkhana on Sunday, and Alex had never pulled a trailer in his life. She'd simply have to haul the horse herself.

Caitlin felt a bit nervous as she hooked up the trailer at Foxwood. Alex had offered to help, but this was something she needed to do on her own. She had to back her truck up to the hitch several times before she got it right, but once she had the hitching mechanism locked down onto the hitch ball, she felt a surge of triumph. Confidently, she towed the empty trailer back to her house.

Alex met her in the driveway. "You did it. I knew you could."

"Thanks." She smiled at him. "It feels weird to be hauling a trailer again. But good."

"Then let's get that horse loaded." He grinned.

"Where's Hallie?" Caitlin zipped her coat against the chill morning.

"Getting Red Fire from his stall." He glanced across the road. "Here she comes."

Hallie, dressed in a cowboy hat, warm coat, black jeans and boots, led the gelding to the trailer. She opened the door and loaded the horse herself.

Caitlin smiled. "Hey, kiddo. I'm proud of you. You're getting to be quite the horsewoman."

"Thanks," Hallie said. She smiled, but it didn't quite reach her eyes. She looked pale.

"Are you feeling okay?" Caitlin wondered if the girl had talked to Alex yet.

"Yeah. I just didn't sleep very well last night. Too excited, I guess."

"Well, that's understandable." Caitlin closed the trailer door and latched it. "Let me see your new shirt."

Hallie unzipped her jacket to expose the peach blouse. She seemed to be maintaining her normal weight. But then, bulimia was hard to spot just by looking. "Looks sharp. You're gonna knock 'em dead." She gave Hallie the thumbs-up.

"Ready?" Alex asked.

"As I'll ever be." Caitlin took a deep breath and slid back behind the wheel. Her hip ached a bit from the cold, but other than that, she felt wonderful. Exhilarated, she backed the trailer out onto the road and headed for Ferguson.

The show was being held at the county fairgrounds, in the recently built indoor arena. Already, several pickup trucks and trailers lined the parking lot. Caitlin found a space and pulled in. "I've rented us a stall," she said. "That way you'll have someplace to put Red Fire between classes, rather than just tie him to the trailer."

"You should've told me," Alex said. "I'll repay you."

"No, you won't." She closed the truck door. "It's my treat."

They found their stall a few minutes later, and Hallie saddled Red Fire, then took him to warm up in the arena before the competition began. She'd be entering ring spearing, flag racing and keyhole. She'd practiced the latest two until she was now able to do them at a fast-paced lope—nearly a gallop. She'd definitely be running barrels by next year.

"I'd better go help Shauna at the registration booth," Caitlin said. "I'll see you later, Alex."

"Hang on a second." He took her by the arm and tugged her toward him. "I didn't get the chance to thank you properly for all you've done for Hallie." He bent and brushed his lips against hers.

Her heart raced. "Alex, there are children present."

"I know," he said in a low tone. He let go of her, his lips curving. "That's the only thing keeping me from ravishing you. See ya." He tipped his hat, all cowboy.

All tall, sexy, long-legged...

Stop it.

His stubbornness toward Hallie's eating disorder was a perfect example of the way things would be between them if they were to become any more seriously involved. He'd made it clear he didn't want anyone mothering his daughter. Not only that, Caitlin had made the decision to go back to school after the holidays were over. She planned to tell Alex after the gymkhana. She would get her degree, then see where things took her. She had to make her own future.

She wanted to explore her options. To see what it was like to stand on her own. And a ready-made family with a stubborn husband didn't take her in that direction.

At the registration booth, things were hectic. Kids and parents lined up to fill out entry forms or turn in preregistration forms. Caitlin stacked forms on the table, recording each person's name on a clipboard, then filing the entry fees and entries away in a lockbox. The classes were divided into age groups, with a novice division open to everyone.

Hallie handed her entry form and money to Caitlin.

"Hey, Hallie. All set?"

"Yeah, but I've got butterflies in my stomach."

Caitlin grinned and wrote her name down. "That comes with the territory. I still get...well, I used to still get them whenever I rode." She glanced at Hallie's entry form to be sure Alex had signed it, then tucked it away in the filing box. "They ease up with time, though."

"Dad's holding Red Fire over by the gate for me. I think he's more nervous than I am."

"I'll bet."

"Any last-minute instructions?" Hallie's eager smile warmed her heart.

"Not really. Just ride him like he's yours. And tell your dad I'll be over in a few minutes, just as soon as all the entries are in."

"Okay. Thanks, Caitlin."

"Oh, hang on. You forgot your change."

But Hallie had sprinted away. Caitlin shrugged. She'd return it to Alex later.

The events began at nine. Caitlin joined Alex by the gate where the contestants were gathered. "Hi. Are you nervous?"

"Me?" he asked. "No way." Then he grinned. "Okay, yes. Very. But I trust Hallie and Red Fire, and you've been a great instructor." He rubbed his knuckles against her cheek. "Thanks again."

"No problem." She walked over to where Hallie sat mounted on Red Fire. "Good luck, kiddo. Remember, it's all for fun."

"I know." Hallie tugged her hat brim down.

The announcer's voice came over the speaker, welcoming everyone to the second annual Sunday Fun Day. Then he announced the opening event—ring spearing—and called out the name of the first contestant, plus the next two in line. Hallie was fourth on the list and, when her turn came, she rode into the arena looking anxious and excited.

She took the long stick to spear the rings—attached to poles along either side of the fence—and set off at a slow lope. She managed to get two of the eight rings and make it back across the finish line at a near-gallop. She grinned as she accepted her time penalty for missing six rings.

Alex patted her knee as she exited the arena. "That's okay, Hal. You did it."

"It was fun," Hallie said. "I'll get more rings next time."

"That's right," Caitlin said. "Good job, Hallie."

They sat outside the arena and watched the other contestants make their runs. Hallie's face fell a little when the ribbons were handed out. Caitlin knew it was disappointing not to get one, even if the girl really hadn't expected to.

Pole bending was next, and Hallie watched from the sidelines. "I want to learn to do that, too," she said.

Her next event was flag racing. She made a clean run, getting both flags in and out of the buckets, though her time wasn't good enough for her to place. But in the novice keyhole, she managed to take Red Fire through the pattern at a slow gallop, and enough of her competitors suffered penalties from downed poles or disqualifications for breaking the pattern, to allow Hallie to place sixth. She accepted the green ribbon with a huge grin.

"Way to go, Hal!" Alex shouted, applauding and whistling.

Caitlin cheered. They met Hallie at the gate. "Look at you," Caitlin said.

"I can't believe it!" Hallie held up the ribbon. "I actually placed." She leaned down to hug Red Fire's neck. "We did it, boy. Here, Dad. Tie this on his bridle." She held out the ribbon, and Alex obliged her, fastening it to Red Fire's headstall just below the gelding's ear.

"Guess that's it, huh?" He patted the chestnut. "Ready to unsaddle your horse?"

"I want to ride him around a little longer and watch the other events," Hallie said.

"Barrels are up next," Caitlin reminded her.

"I know. I want to watch up close, so I thought I'd sit on Red Fire by the arena. Okay, Dad?"

"All right. Just be careful." Alex grinned as he watched her trot away.

"Alex," Caitlin said, "did you notice how flushed she looked?"

"'Course she did. She just won her first ribbon."

"No, it's more than that. This morning I thought she looked pale and tired when we loaded up for the show."

He sighed. "Yeah, I noticed that, too. As a matter of fact, you'll be happy to know I've got a doctor's appointment scheduled for Tuesday."

"Really?" Caitlin's spirits soared.

"Yes. Satisfied?"

"Thank you, Alex."

"I still don't think she's bulimic," he said, "but I am wondering if she might need vitamins or something."

"Maybe." He was obviously still in denial, and without him alerting Hallie's physician, she wasn't so sure the doctor's visit would help much. She only hoped the doctor would attribute her haggard appearance and bloodshot eyes to something more than exhaustion.

The arena crew had cleared out the keyhole poles and now had the barrels set in place. "Come on," Caitlin said. "Let's get a seat for this one. It's my favorite."

They found a spot to squeeze into on the bleachers, and Caitlin focused on the floor. "That'll be Hallie out there next year," she said.

Alex grinned. "No doubt."

They watched the junior, senior and adult classes run the course, the first-place trophy and subsequent ribbons handed out after each division.

The announcer's voice boomed over the loudspeaker. "Up next, we have the novice barrel racing, ladies and gentlemen. You won't want to miss this. Our first rider is Hallie Hunter from Deer Creek, riding Red Fire. Put your hands together for this little lady."

"What?!" With a gasp, Caitlin rose to her feet.

"What the hell—?" Alex was already moving down the bleachers to the floor.

Lord, no. Caitlin hurried after him, her heart

pounding. Hallie had no idea what she was getting into. Red Fire would take one look at the cloverleaf pattern and be off like a rocket.

"Hallie, no!" Alex shouted.

Too late. She was already in the arena, the gate man swinging the gate shut behind her. Alex vaulted onto the fence, but one of the ring crew members stopped him. The two exchanged heated words.

Caitlin didn't bother to listen. She hurried as fast as she could, around the fence near the starting line. "Hallie!" she called. "Stop. Now!"

Briefly, Hallie met her gaze as Red Fire danced in place, eager to run. "I can do it!" Hallie said. She leaned forward in the saddle, putting slack in the reins, and Caitlin's heart nearly stopped as Red Fire shot forward.

Hallie snapped backward with the unexpected force of the gelding's momentum, nearly losing her balance. But she managed to grab the saddle horn and cling to it. "Whoa!" she shouted, pulling up on the reins.

Red Fire barely slowed. With a shake of his head, he plunged toward the first barrel. Caitlin ducked through the fence.

"Whoa!" she called, knowing it wouldn't do much good, but trying anyway. She ignored the ring crew as they motioned for her to clear the area. Alex had scrambled over the fence, as well.

Everything happened in seconds.

But it felt like an eternity.

Red Fire dropped into the turn with lightning speed, and Hallie slumped, then fell. The crowd let out a collective gasp, and several crew members hurried toward her.

Alex reached her first. "Hallie!" He knelt beside her.

The metal barrel had been knocked over, but he wasn't sure if Red Fire had hit it or Hallie.

"Dear God. Hallie." All the blood drained from Alex's face as he held his daughter in his arms. She was out cold, her face white as a sheet.

The on-site paramedics cleared the area, forcing everyone to move back while they tended to Hallie. Alex hovered at their elbows, obviously torn between giving them room and being with his little girl.

He caught Caitlin's gaze. "What was she doing? Did you tell her she could ride in the barrel race?"

"Of course not."

"Then how did this happen?" He craned his neck, trying to get a good look at Hallie. She lay on a backboard on the gurney.

Caitlin's mind whirled. "She brought her entry form to me, but—" She suddenly remembered the extra money. No wonder Hallie hadn't waited for her change. Caitlin could've kicked herself for not looking closer at Hallie's form. She must have filled in the box to enter barrels after Alex signed it.

The paramedics lifted the gurney and hustled Hallie out to the waiting ambulance. "I'm going with her," Alex said.

"They won't let you ride in the ambulance," Caitlin explained. "Here." She handed him her truck keys. "I'm shaking so hard, I don't think I can drive." She raced with him to the parking lot.

"Caitlin, hold up!" Shauna called. "Is Hallie okay?"

"I don't know," Caitlin said over her shoulder.

Shauna hurried to catch up. "How did this happen? I didn't think Hallie was entered in the barrel racing."

"She wasn't," Caitlin said. "I'll call you later, Shauna. I've got to run." She climbed into the Chevy and Alex sped toward the hospital.

ALEX GRIPPED the steering wheel, blowing his horn as he dodged in and out of Sunday traffic on the highway. He felt like all the air had been knocked from his lungs.

Hallie's face had been so pale. *Dear God, if anything happened to her...*

He couldn't even finish the thought.

At the hospital, he approached a nurse in the emergency-room waiting area. "My daughter was brought in by the ambulance. I need to see her."

"Have a seat, sir—"

"I don't want a seat, damn it! I want my little girl."

"Alex." Caitlin laid her hand on his arm. "Come on. They need a few minutes to work on her."

"You'll be allowed in the exam room shortly, sir," the nurse said. "In the meantime, we'll need some information from you, if you'll step over to the desk." She pointed.

Alex could barely give his name to the woman at check-in. The siren still echoed in his head.

Sirens, wailing down the street.

An everyday sound. He'd thought nothing of it when they passed by his house.

Then the phone call. The ambulance arriving at Humana Hospital—too late to help Melissa.

Please, God, please don't take my little girl.

"Alex," Caitlin said softly. "If you don't breathe, they're going to lay you out in the room next to her."

He looked up to where she stood beside the chair he'd been forced to sit in. "I can't lose her," he whispered. "I can't."

"You won't." Caitlin gripped his hand. "She's going to be fine."

"Mr. Hunter?" A woman in blue scrubs called his name. "You can come back now."

He rushed forward, Caitlin right behind. Hallie lay on a gurney, nearly as pale as the pillow beneath her head. But she was awake.

"Dad," she said. "Caitlin. I'm sorry."

"Hallie." He breathed her name. With both his hands, he cradled her hand. It felt soft and small.

"Baby, you scared me half to death." He kissed her knuckles, then pressed her hand against his cheek.

"Mr. Hunter?" An older man in a white coat held his hand out to Alex. "I'm Doctor Flinner." He shook Caitlin's hand, as well, assuming she was Hallie's mother.

Alex didn't bother to correct him. "Is Hallie all right?"

"Other than a small bump on the head and some low blood sugar, she's fine." He smiled at Hallie. "Your daughter tells me she skipped breakfast this morning."

Alex frowned. He'd made muffins and sliced up some cantaloupe, nothing too heavy on her stomach. But she'd been so excited, he'd had a hard time getting her to sit at the table. She'd promised to eat while he showered, and when he'd come back into the kitchen, she'd already cleared the dishes and gone out to take care of Red Fire.

"Hal?"

She squirmed. "I was too excited about the gymkhana."

"She has a minor concussion," Dr. Flinner went on. "But I don't think it was the head injury that caused her to black out. I'd say low blood sugar—possibly coupled with anemia—is the culprit. We'll draw some blood, take a couple of X-rays, and she can be on her way."

"Thank you, Doctor." Relief washed over him. Doctor Flinner left the room, and Alex sat on the edge of the gurney. "Do you want to tell me how this happened?"

Hallie looked sheepish. "I told you. I skipped breakfast."

"Hal." He gave her a firm look.

"O-kay." She sighed. "I thought I could do the barrels, since Red Fire knows what he's doing. I wanted to surprise you and Caitlin."

"I'd say you did that all right," Caitlin said. "Good Lord, kiddo, you scared the life out of me." Just then, her cell phone rang. "Shoot, I meant to shut that off. Excuse me. I need to go outside to answer it." She hurried out the door.

"I didn't enter you in the barrels," Alex said.

"I marked it off on the checklist after you signed," Hallie said. "I used my own money."

That irritated him. "Who took your entry form?"

"Caitlin did. But, Dad, don't get mad at her. I kept her talking so she wouldn't notice."

He pressed his lips together. "I guess I don't need to lecture you."

"No." She wrinkled her nose. "I think that whack on the head is good enough."

Caitlin returned a few moments later. "It was Shauna. She looked at Hallie's entry form—"

"I already told him," Hallie said.

"What were you thinking?"

"I wanted to impress you."

"Looks like the only impression you made was on your noggin," Alex said. "Hal, don't ever lie like that again."

"Don't worry. I won't." She gave him an impish grin. "At least, not until next year."

A nurse and an orderly hustled into the room and whisked Hallie off to radiology. Alex sank into a chair beside Caitlin.

She looked at him, her expression solemn. "Alex, I don't think she fell off Red Fire."

"What do you mean?"

"She fainted. And it wasn't from not eating breakfast." Her blue eyes held his.

"She admitted she didn't eat this morning." Irritated, he bit the words off. "Why are you so determined to make something out of nothing? Don't you think the doctor would know if something was out of the ordinary?"

"Bulimia isn't easy to detect. Not like anorexia. Hallie looks normal weight. But she has other symptoms, and if you bring them to the doctor's attention, he'll know what to look for."

"He said she has low blood sugar."

Caitlin rose from her chair. "I can't do this anymore, Alex. I'll be out in the parking lot."

She turned and walked out of the room.

CHAPTER SIXTEEN

CAITLIN PACKED her clothes in the suitcase she'd laid on the bed. She'd called Alex earlier to check up on Hallie, and he'd been polite but distant. The same way he'd been on their drive home from the hospital. Hallie's X-rays had turned up clean, but the results of her blood work wouldn't be back until tomorrow. The information would be sent to her doctor so he'd have it to review in time for her Tuesday appointment.

Alex could stick his head in the sand all he wanted. She knew Hallie had fainted. Of course, it wasn't likely she would've been able to bring Red Fire under control anyway. But Caitlin was sure it was the weakness from the bulimia that had actually caused her fall from the horse. And for that, she blamed Alex.

She needed time and space away from him. If he was bound and determined to be an ignorant fool, risking his daughter's health and life...well, she didn't have to stand around and watch. Her parents had planned a ski trip to Aspen over the next few days. They'd leave tomorrow. She couldn't do the slopes anymore, but she could at least relax in the lodge. Maybe it would help clear her mind.

Maybe Alex would listen to her mother, since she'd raised two children and had seen eating disorders firsthand.

What an idiot she'd been. Hell, she'd started to believe she might be falling in love with Alex.

Ha!

Once she got back from Aspen, she might as well stay at Foxwood until after the holidays. She would pack up the few things she had here, and leave her furniture for later. Her rent was paid up through the first of the year.

When the holidays were over, she'd head for Fort Collins. She'd get her degree, get on with her life and forget she'd ever known Alex Hunter.

ALEX FROWNED as he looked across the road. Caitlin had said very little to him as they returned to the fairgrounds to pick up Red Fire. He'd expected her to take the horse trailer back to Foxwood, but there it was, still in her driveway. And as he watched, she came out of her barn leading Silver Fox, then loaded him into the trailer.

What the hell?

He started to call out to her, to go over and ask what she was doing. But he was still ticked off by the remark she'd made in the emergency room.

I can't do this anymore, Alex.

Do what? Interfere? Have hot sex with him while his daughter was at school?

He felt ashamed. He'd been smitten with Caitlin to the point of acting like a randy teenager. His midday rendezvous with her was something he'd definitely looked forward to. He'd thought they had something going...something good.

He watched her get into the truck with Spike and pull away. She'd left no lights on in the house—just in the yard. She must be taking Silver Fox back to Foxwood. But why? The last he'd heard, she planned to bring Black Knight over to keep Fox company. Apparently she'd changed her mind. Maybe Hallie's episode with the barrel race had made Caitlin decide to give up on horses. He wished she'd stop blaming herself for what had happened.

Back in the house, Alex fixed chicken noodle soup and grilled cheese sandwiches and ate with Hallie in the living room, where they watched a comedy video. He'd told her she could stay home from school the next day, but she'd insisted she was fine. After the movie, she headed for bed. Alex did the dishes, then spent the night tossing and turning, unable to get Caitlin off his mind.

The next morning he prepared oatmeal and bran muffins for Hallie, making a note to pick up some vitamins. Once she'd boarded the school bus, he headed for his computer. He needed to get his mind back on work and quit thinking about Caitlin. Her truck still wasn't in the driveway.

But the papers she'd given him were there on his desk. He hadn't meant to leave them out where Hallie might see them. He scooped them up and started to chuck them into the trash can.

But something Caitlin had marked with a yellow highlighter stood out on the top page. *Warning signs of bulimia:*

Makes excuses to go to the bathroom after meals.

Has mood swings, oftentimes depression.

Weight may be in normal range.

Frequently eats large amounts of food on the spur of the moment, often in secret.

He sat down—hard—and read some more. And found out that bulimia rarely shows up in lab tests for blood and urine.

He thought about the way Hallie packed away enormous amounts of food. And he thought about her mood swings, which he'd attributed to Melissa's death. When he'd found her coming down the staircase at the Kramers' on Thanksgiving, he'd thought she'd been snooping. But had she gone looking for another bathroom, one not so close to the dining room?

By the time he was finished reading the stack of papers Caitlin had given him, Alex was shaking. *Dear God. Was it really possible?*

Could he be so blind?

Fear mounting, he filed away facts on the complications caused by bulimia. Weakness, exhaustion and bloodshot eyes. Tooth erosion. Ruptures of the stomach and esophagus from repeated vomiting. Irregular heartbeat and in severe cases heart attack.

Setting the papers back on his desk, Alex went into Hallie's room. Her bed was haphazardly made, an ancient teddy bear centered on the pillow. All around him were signs of his little girl growing up. Amid the posters on the walls of horses were those of boy bands, some of the guys shirtless. He spotted a single tube of the pale pink lipstick he allowed her to wear occasionally, lying on the rug near the bed.

He picked it up and set it on the dresser. Taking a deep breath, he began to go through her things. He felt like an intruder, but he told himself it was his job as a parent to do this. He really had no idea what he was looking for. Just something—anything—that might disprove what he'd read.

He dug through Hallie's dresser drawers, finding nothing out of the ordinary, other than a spoon. Then he started on the closet. The first thing he found was a bag of chocolate chip cookies, tucked away on the top shelf. And another of cheese puffs. Where had they come from? He hadn't bought them. He continued to dig, riffling through her clothes, poking around on the shelves. He found a shoebox and opened the lid.

Frowning, he lifted out a pottery bowl. *What the hell?* His blood ran cold as he looked at it. A girl's face was painted on the side, tears falling in black dots from her eyes. And in red letters, there were words circling the rim of the bowl....

Control, relief, peace. There was also a crude rendition of a girl, lying on her back among headstones.

Had Hallie made this? And if so, when? Where? A million questions raced through his mind as he carried it into the living room. He knew what the bowl was for. He'd read the literature.

Alex set the purging bowl on the coffee table and sank onto the couch.

Where had he gone wrong? He'd tried so hard to be a good father. He'd given Hallie all his love and attention and everything she could ever need. Except a mother. Was that why she'd turned to this? The literature he'd read indicated emotional trauma could be a trigger. Or peer pressure. Or genetic factors.

He raked his hands through his hair.

He'd done his best to protect his daughter, especially after Melissa was killed. He'd bought this house and moved her out of the city. He'd hovered over her, and worried about her getting hurt riding horses or walking to a friend's house. And he'd even worried that Caitlin would do something to hurt her.

As it turned out Caitlin had been a godsend, and he'd been too stupid to see it.

He'd protected Hallie from all outside forces. The one thing he couldn't protect Hallie from was herself.

HALLIE GOT OFF the bus and looked over at Caitlin's. Her truck still wasn't in the driveway. It hadn't been there when she'd left for school this morning, either. Where had she been all day? Maybe she should surprise Caitlin and feed Silver Fox for her. Make up for the stupid stunt she'd pulled at the gymkhana.

After crossing the road, Hallie set her backpack down by the barn door and went inside. "Silver Fox?" He wasn't in his stall, and she hadn't seen him outside. She went through the rear entrance to the paddock. The gate stood open, leading to the pasture. He must be out there somewhere. She whistled. "Come on, Fox! I've got horse cookies." Nothing.

Where was he? Puzzled, Hallie walked back around to the front of the barn. She paused, listening. Normally, Spike would bark at her. Caitlin must've taken him with her. Walking through the yard to the back door, Hallie knocked on the off chance she was here. Maybe Caitlin's brother had borrowed her truck. Or her dad. He'd done that last time, when their Ranger wouldn't run. But she knew he'd be at home when she got off the school bus.

When her knock went unanswered, Hallie cupped

her hands around her face and peered through the window. She caught her breath. The few knickknacks and photographs that had lined the shelves and tables were all gone, as was the mirror that had hung on the wall near the dining area. Except for Caitlin's furniture, it was empty. No books. No sign of Spike's toys. Panicked, Hallie ran around to the bedroom window. The closet stood open, empty, and the bed had been stripped.

Surely Caitlin wouldn't leave. Not without saying goodbye. And why?

Suddenly, Hallie knew the answer. It was because of her. What she'd done. She'd upset Caitlin by breaking her trust. No wonder she'd acted so strange when they'd driven home from the hospital.

Hallie wandered back out to the barn. The hay was still there. Maybe that was a good thing. But she knew it was only because no one had come yet to pick it up. That was probably the same reason Caitlin's furniture was still in the house.

Tears burned her eyes and clogged her throat.

Sinking down beside the haystack, Hallie let them come.

ALEX HEARD the school bus and held his breath. This wasn't going to be easy. But the minutes ticked by, and Hallie didn't come inside. She must've gone to feed Red Fire and Splash. Sometimes she did that the minute she got home. He treasured the love Hallie had for the horses. Maybe he could use that as a means of getting through to her. She couldn't ride if she was sick.

Dear God, why hadn't he listened to Caitlin?

Twenty minutes passed. Still no sign of Hallie. She had to have gotten off the bus. He'd heard it stop, and she was the only kid who lived here. What if she'd fainted again? Putting on his coat, he went outside. She wasn't in the barn, and the horses hadn't been fed. Heart pounding, Alex hurried back toward the yard. "Hallie!" *Where was she?*

He went across the road, even though Caitlin's truck still wasn't in the driveway. The barn door was open. "Hallie?"

"In here."

He could tell by her voice she'd been crying. He found her sitting at the bottom of the haystack. "Hal, what's wrong?"

"Caitlin's gone and it's all my fault. If I hadn't been so stupid then I wouldn't have fainted and she wouldn't be mad at me and she'd be here."

"What? Honey, slow down." He wiped the tears from her cheeks. "Caitlin's not mad at you."

"Yes, she is. She must be, or she wouldn't have left without saying goodbye."

"She'll be home later. It's no big deal."

"No, she won't. Her stuff is all gone."

"What?"

"I looked in the windows. All her pictures and things are gone. Just the furniture's left."

He was speechless. Why would Caitlin move out so abruptly? "Surely not, honey. If her furniture's still there, then there's probably some other reason why her stuff isn't." But he couldn't think of a single one. She'd taken her things, her horse, and driven away. Obviously, she'd gone back to Foxwood. And that could only mean one thing.

She'd left to get away from him.

"I didn't mean to screw everything up," Hallie said, sniffing.

"You didn't, honey. Come on." He tugged her gently to her feet, angry that Caitlin would take off without a word to Hallie, or him either for that matter. "It's cold out here. Let's go home and feed the horses, then make some hot chocolate. We'll call Caitlin, and you can talk to her and see for yourself that she's not mad at you. Okay?"

She nodded. His mind whirled as they took care of Red Fire and Splash. He had more important things to deal with than Caitlin. How should he approach Hallie?

He didn't have to wonder long. Her eyes fell on the purging bowl the minute she entered the living room. It sat there on the coffee table, its presence dominating the room. Hallie's gaze met his, and for the first time he realized she looked more than tired. Her eyes were bloodshot, with dark circles underneath. Why hadn't he noticed?

He'd been too wound up in what he felt for Caitlin, and too stubborn to admit that he was wrong about his daughter.

Hallie's lip trembled, and her eyes welled up. "Oh, great, Dad! Just great. Now you're raiding my room?" She turned and fled, slamming the bedroom door behind her.

"Hallie, open the door." He knocked firmly on it, then tried the knob. She'd locked it. "We need to talk, honey, and I love you enough to take this door off its hinges if that's what it takes."

Silence.

"All right. I'll be back with my tools."

He heard her flip the lock open. She swung the door wide, scowling. "You might as well come in. You've already ransacked the place."

"Hal, I didn't touch anything I didn't have to."

"Why?" Her eyes searched his accusingly. "Why couldn't you just talk to me? Why did you have to invade my privacy, Dad? Jeez."

"Because I care." He slipped his arms around her and drew her into a hug. "I've let you down, Hal."

She pulled back, looking up at him suspiciously. "What do you mean?"

"Caitlin noticed something was wrong long be-

fore I did. She tried to tell me, but I wouldn't listen."
He brushed her hair back from her face. "You're all
I've got, and I'd do anything for you. You know that,
don't you?"

She nodded.

"Then talk to me, baby."

She bit her lip. "I'm scared, Dad."

"So am I. But we can deal with this thing together.
Just like we always do."

"I don't know where to start."

"Why don't you tell me about your purging bowl,"
he said. "And then we'll go over some papers together."

"What papers?"

"Some stuff Caitlin printed off the Internet."

Hallie looked upset. "Great. She probably thinks
I'm a real loser."

"Hardly. She cares about you, too. A lot. She's
been really worried, and she wants to help."

"Then why did she leave?"

"I don't know. But as soon as we get done talking, we'll call her and find out."

CAITLIN STOOD at the living room window of the ski
lodge, staring out at the distant slopes. The ever-
greens and aspen were blanketed in snow, and the
sun made a feeble attempt to cut through the late
afternoon clouds. Her parents and Dillon were still
out skiing. Gran had chosen not to join them this trip.

She had a new man in her life—a retired horse trainer—and they'd made other plans for the week.

She was surprised, therefore, when the phone rang and Gran's voice came over the line. "Hi, honey. How are things in Aspen?"

"Cold but gorgeous. Is everything okay, Gran?"

"Perfect. Henry's here, and we're getting ready to go to Buffalo Valley for some steaks and a little dancing."

"Sounds fun."

"I noticed you forgot to take your cell phone with you." Gran's voice bore a note of mock scolding.

"No, I didn't." Caitlin slid onto a stool at the breakfast bar and twirled the phone cord around her finger. "I didn't think I'd need it, considering Mom, Dad and Dillon all have theirs."

"Well, I didn't want to give Alex the number to the condo without asking you first."

"Alex?"

"Yes. You remember…that handsome young man who's sweet on you?"

"Gran."

"He called here for you, and when I told him you'd gone to the ski lodge, he asked for your cell number. Of course, you'd left your phone on the kitchen table, so I told him I'd give you the message and have you call him." She paused. "Honey, I could hear it in his voice. He really wants to talk to you. I almost went ahead and gave him the number for the lodge, I felt so sorry for the poor boy."

"I appreciate that you didn't, Gran. I don't want to talk to him right now."

"I think you're making a mistake."

"With all due respect, Gran, I don't."

"Well, it's your life. But if I were you, I'd call him back. I've got to run, dear. Henry's waiting. Give everyone my love, and have fun."

"You, too, Gran." Caitlin hung up the phone. What was Alex doing calling Foxwood? He must've noticed she wasn't home; that she'd taken Silver Fox. A sudden thought flew into her head. *Hallie.* What if something was wrong? What if she'd gotten worse, or there'd been residual effects from the head injury. Caitlin picked up the phone and dialed.

"Hello?"

"Alex, it's Caitlin. Is everything all right? Is Hallie okay?"

"Yes and no."

"What's wrong?"

He was silent a moment. "I found a purging bowl in her room."

"Oh, Alex." She slumped in her chair, torn between relief and regret. Maybe now he'd get Hallie the help she needed. "How did you know what it was?"

"I finally read your research."

"Have you talked to her about it?"

"Oh, yeah. We had a long talk. Hallie's agreed to discuss things with her doctor tomorrow when we go to her appointment. She's scared, Caitlin. She admitted her...bulimia has gotten way beyond her control."

Caitlin squeezed her eyes shut. "I'm glad you're getting help for her."

"She's upset that you're gone."

Feeling guilty, she paced. "I needed some space, Alex. I'm at our ski condo in Aspen."

"That's what your grandmother said."

She took a deep breath. "I only wanted to be sure everything was okay with Hallie."

"She looked in your windows, Caitlin. She said your things are gone. And I saw you load Silver Fox into the horse trailer last night. What's going on?"

"I brought him back to Foxwood."

"Why?"

She told herself she had to do this. Had to stick to her guns. "I'm going to stay there through the holidays. Then I'm going back to CSU."

He was silent for a moment. "I see. So, that's it? You just left without saying goodbye?"

"I'd planned to call Hallie later." *I wanted to call you.*

"I'm sure she'd rather see you."

She couldn't do it. Couldn't face him right now.

Just because Alex had finally seen the light of day about his daughter…

"Can you put Hallie on the phone, please?"

"Yeah. I'll get her." He set the phone down with a clunk that made her start.

A few moments later, Hallie's voice came on the line. "Hey, Caitlin."

"Hi, kiddo. How are you?"

"I'm okay." But her voice said otherwise.

Dear Lord. She couldn't just abandon the child. "Your dad tells me you're seeing your doctor tomorrow."

"That's right."

"I hope you know, Hallie, you've got nothing to be ashamed of."

"I guess."

"I'm proud of you."

"Proud? I thought you were mad at me."

"Now why would I be mad at my favorite kid?"

"Because of what I did at the gymkhana."

"I'm not mad. Just worried about you."

"But you moved out of your house."

"That has nothing to do with you, sweetie." She paused. "Tell you what. I'll be staying here in Aspen for a few days, then I'll be back at Foxwood. How about if you come out for a visit on the weekend?"

"Really?"

"Sure. You can even bring your grumpy old dad."

She didn't want to face Alex in his house. Or in her near-vacant one. "You can see how big the foals have grown, and if it snows we'll take you on that sleigh ride you missed out on Thanksgiving Day."

"Okay." She sounded somewhat cheered.

"Hey, if you need me, call anytime, all right?" She gave Hallie the number to the condo, just to be sure, and to her cell phone for later. "Put your dad back on, kiddo."

"Okay. Bye."

Caitlin took a deep breath as Alex came back on the line. "I invited Hallie out to Foxwood this weekend. Will you bring her?"

"I suppose."

"We can talk then."

"Fine."

"How about Saturday...say around noon?"

"We'll be there."

They said their goodbyes and Caitlin hung up, then sat staring at the phone. She'd been in denial.

Saying goodbye to Hallie wouldn't be easy.

But it was going to be even harder to say goodbye to Alex.

CHAPTER SEVENTEEN

PATCHES OF SNOW lay melting on the road as Alex drove Hallie toward Foxwood. He couldn't wait to tell Caitlin the good news from Hallie's doctor. On the other hand, he hated the thought of saying goodbye to her. She'd made it plain she didn't plan to return to the farm. She'd graduate from CSU, and then what?

Do the same damned thing he needed to do. Get on with her life.

He told himself it didn't matter. He and Hallie had each other, just like they'd always had. They didn't need anyone else. But the minute he laid eyes on Caitlin, he knew he'd been lying.

She stood on the massive porch of the gated estate, looking every inch the lady. She wore jeans and the same red sweater he'd seen her in that day at Pearl's Diner. The sweater that suited her complexion and her pretty, dark hair. He wanted to touch her. Wanted to sweep her into his arms and kiss her and hold her and never let her go.

He loved her.

And he wished she could love him back. But if she was going to walk away from him—right out of his life—then the least he could do was let her go with his head held high.

She greeted Hallie with a smile, but her eyes included him. "How's it going, kiddo?"

"Pretty good." Hallie's color looked better than it had a week ago. Alex had her on a healthy diet and vitamins, and she was seeing a therapist. One who specialized in eating disorders.

He didn't know what to say to Caitlin. Hands stuck in his front pockets, he shuffled his feet. "It's good to see you."

"You, too."

"How's Silver Fox?" Hallie asked.

"Doing great. And Red Fire?"

"He's fine." Hallie eyed her warily. "Are you going to bring him back here to Foxwood?"

"Certainly not. Why would I?"

Hallie's mouth turned down at the corners. "I don't know. I just figured, with you going off to school and all, you'd want him back."

Caitlin placed her hands on Hallie's shoulders, looking her square in the eye. "Red Fire's not going anywhere," she said. "He's your horse now."

"Wha-at?"

"You heard me." She looked up at Alex, as if to say, *I hope this is all right with you.*

He smothered a chuckle. If not, it was too late anyway. The look on his daughter's face was priceless.

"But I thought you said you could never part with him."

"I didn't think I could. But it's obvious that you love him just as much as I do. I think he'd be happier belonging to you. After all, he loves to barrel race."

Hallie blushed, then laughed. "Sorry about the dumb stunt I pulled."

"I told you before—no worries. Now come on, let's go see the foals."

Alex followed along behind them, to the pasture where the weanlings stood, picking at the grass through patches of snow. They'd grown considerably, their long legs like stilts on hooves. Caitlin got a bucket from the barn and filled it with sweet grain, then handed it to Hallie. "Go ahead. Give them a treat. They'll be your pals for life."

Hallie dashed away, literally in horse heaven.

Alex leaned on the fence next to Caitlin. "When are you leaving?" he asked.

"The Sunday after New Year's Day. I want to be in my dorm room that morning. That way I can get settled in and have a good night's sleep before classes start."

"Sounds like a plan." He stood there, a thousand

emotions churning inside. How had he so misjudged what was happening between them?

"Hallie looks a little better," Caitlin said. "How's she coming along?"

"Her doctor and therapist told me it's lucky she was diagnosed fairly early. She's only been binging and purging since Melissa's death. We expect her to make a full recovery."

"That's the best news I've heard all year," she said. She smiled up at him. "Alex, I—"

"Caitlin, I'm—"

She laughed. "Go ahead."

"I'm sorry I was so stubborn. That I didn't listen to you. I was scared."

"I know."

"I thought I was protecting Hallie."

"I know that, too. I'm sorry I upset you."

"Don't be. If you hadn't been so pushy, I might never have gotten Hallie the help she needs."

"I don't know about that." She gave him a cocky grin. "You are pretty stubborn."

"Yeah, I am." And suddenly, he knew what he needed to say to her. He couldn't let her leave without telling her exactly what was on his mind—in his heart. "Do you know why I started pushing you away?"

"I made you mad?"

"No. I was scared."

"What do you mean?"

He slipped his arms around her waist. "I kept telling myself it was for Hallie. That I didn't want to see her hurt anymore—abandoned by yet another person."

She chewed her bottom lip. "And here I am, doing just that…at least in her eyes."

"Maybe. But we'll deal with it. The point is, I was scared of being hurt myself." He brushed his knuckles against her cheek. "You're the only woman I've cared about in a long, long time. I was afraid of losing that."

"You mean those nooners were all just to be sure I stuck around?"

He chuckled. "Maybe, in part. But seriously, I hated the thought of you going your own way and leaving me behind. And now you are, and I don't know what to do about it." He took a deep breath, then took the plunge. "I love you, Caitlin."

Her eyes widened, then softened. "I love you, too, you stubborn cowboy." She smacked his shoulders with the palms of her hands, his arms still locked around her. "Are you really that dense? Did you really think I was leaving for good?"

He lifted a shoulder. "You packed all your things."

"Only because my lease is coming up on the farm the first of the year. There was no sense in paying to keep it while I was away at CSU. But I planned to come back to Foxwood after I graduate."

"And then what?"

She sobered. "I honestly didn't know, Alex. I just figured I'd take things one day at a time."

"And when were you going to tell me you loved me?"

"As soon as I got up the nerve."

"Hey, you two!" Hallie rushed to the fence and slid between the rails, the grain bucket empty in her hand. "What, are you going all mushy on me—saying goodbye?"

"And what if we are?" Caitlin asked, frowning.

Hallie pressed her lips together. "Actually, I'm glad to see it."

"Is that right?" Caitlin smiled.

"Yeah." Hallie swallowed. "I was afraid you'd go away to Fort Collins and never come back."

Caitlin pulled out of Alex's arms and faced his daughter. "No way. I promised I'd teach you to barrel race, didn't I?"

"Yeah." Hallie's eyes suddenly teared up. "Please don't ever leave us for good, Caitlin. You—you're like a mom to me."

Alex watched the change in Caitlin's expression. Her features shifted, melted, and her eyes grew moist. "Me?" She pointed at herself. "A mom?"

"I know. It's dumb, huh?"

"No. It's not dumb at all." She took hold of Hallie's arms. "It's the most wonderful thing I've ever heard. It's better than a gold medal."

"Really?"

Caitlin hugged her. "You'd better know it."

"So you promise you'll be back?" Hallie asked, as Caitlin let go of her.

"Cross my heart and hope to ride in a blizzard if I don't."

Hallie giggled. "Okay, then." She held up the empty bucket. "Can I give the foals a little more grain?"

"Sure. You know where it is."

Hallie took off.

"Thanks," Alex said.

"For what?"

"For making her happy."

"She's the one who made me happy." Caitlin grinned. "Me. A mom. That is so sweet. I never thought I was cut out to be a mother. But I love your daughter, Alex. I really do."

He held her again. "Will you, then? Be her mother?"

"Sure. If she wants to think of me that way, that's okay by me."

"You're not getting what I'm saying."

She swallowed hard. "I guess I'm afraid to."

"Don't be." He leaned his forehead against hers. "Will you take this ol' cowboy wannabe?" he whispered. "To love and kick butt from now 'til all eternity?"

"Is that a proposal?"

"You'd better know it." Her words. Then he kissed her. "Say you'll marry me, Caitlin."

"I'll marry you, Caitlin."

He grinned. "Smart-ass." Then he held her tight and kissed her over and over again.

EPILOGUE

THE INVITATION came in the mail on the first Saturday in May. Hallie jumped up and down with excitement when Alex showed it to her. Caitlin's graduation ceremony would mark her last day in Fort Collins. Then she'd be coming home to Deer Creek.

Only not to her house.

The wedding was planned for midsummer. Caitlin thought June might be nice—the traditional bride's month. Alex personally didn't care. He'd stand up with a J.P. in the middle of the courthouse with her, just to make her his.

The four-and-a-half-hour drive to Fort Collins seemed endless. He sat next to Hallie in the school stadium, watching proudly as Caitlin accepted her diploma. She'd be putting her animal science degree to good use, raising the quarter horses they planned to buy. After all, good barrel horses brought top dollar. And decent instructors were hard to come by.

After an early celebration dinner, they headed back to Deer Creek. For Hallie's sake, they wouldn't be living under one roof until after the wedding, so Caitlin drove on to Foxwood with a promise to meet them at his place early the next morning.

Alex woke up before the sun was up and headed out to the barn with Hallie, where they saddled the three horses. Dillon had brought Silver Fox a few days ago along with Black Knight. Alex hoped Caitlin would be ready for what he had in mind.

The red truck pulled into his driveway just as the sun was coming up. He stood, holding his horse's reins, watching the woman he loved. She stepped out of the pickup, then folded herself into his arms. He held her and kissed her, loving the way his engagement ring looked on her hand.

"Welcome home, darlin'," he said.

"Those are the sweetest words I've ever heard." She kissed him again, then eyed his horse. "Where's Hallie? You two weren't going riding, were you? It's so early. Besides, I've got a surprise for her."

"She's coming." Alex glanced over at the barn.

Hallie came out, leading Silver Fox and Red Fire. "Hi, Caitlin." She hurried forward, trotting both horses behind her.

"Hey, kiddo. What are you doing with my horse?"

Hallie shrugged. "Dad and I thought maybe it was time."

"For what?" But her lips twitched.

"For you to get back on."

Caitlin laughed, the sound full of joy. "I think he's right. But hang on a second. I've got something for you." She hurried back to her truck and opened the door. Spike bounded out, barking excitedly, and Red Fire pinned his ears at the little dog, then remembered his manners when Hallie spoke softly to him.

Caitlin scooped something into her arms.

"A puppy!" Hallie shrieked and thrust the reins of both bridles into Alex's hands, then rushed to meet Caitlin. "He's so cute. What kind is he?"

"She," Caitlin said, handing the puppy over, "is a genuine, certified mutt. Mom and Gran adopted her from the animal shelter."

The little black-and-tan dog squirmed and wriggled, lapping at Hallie's face with her eager pink tongue.

"I love her! Thank you, Caitlin."

Alex rolled his eyes. "There go all my boots."

Caitlin laughed. "Guess you'll learn to put them up in the closet."

"I guess so. Hallie, why don't you put Spike and your puppy in the yard. We've got some riding to do."

"Oh, all right." Hallie reluctantly locked both dogs in the new fenced-in front yard. "Come on, Caitlin. Let's go."

Caitlin took a deep breath. She looked at Alex.

"You can do it," he said. "I'm here for you. Always." He laced his hands together to give her a leg up.

"I know." She raised her left foot—with a bit of effort—and set it squarely in his hands. Then she swung up onto Silver Fox's back and put both feet in the stirrups. Triumphantly, she gathered her reins. "God, I feel like I'm on top of the world."

He knew she wasn't talking about how tall her horse was.

"So do I, Caitlin. So do I."

He mounted up and the three of them headed down the road, their horses' hooves clopping against the dirt shoulder.

Riding off into the sunrise.

HARLEQUIN *Super*ROMANCE®

ANOTHER WOMAN'S SON
by Anna Adams

Harlequin Superromance #1294

**The truth should set you free.
Sometimes it just tightens the trap.**

Three months ago Isabel Barker's life came crashing
down after her husband confessed he loved another
woman—Isabel's sister—and that they'd had a son
together. No one else, including her sister's husband,
Ben, knows the truth about the baby. When her sister
and her husband are killed, Tony is left with Ben,
and Isabel wonders whether she should tell the truth.
She knows Ben will never forgive her if her honesty
costs him his son.

*Available in August 2005
wherever Harlequin books are sold.*

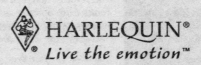
HARLEQUIN®
Live the emotion™

If you enjoyed what you just read,
then we've got an offer you can't resist!

Take 2 bestselling love stories FREE!
Plus get a FREE surprise gift!

"Maybe you ought to go over there and ask her if she's Caitlin Kramer."

But Alex knew it wasn't a good idea. The woman in the wheelchair at the other table seemed uncomfortable in her surroundings...any fool could see that.

"Nah." Hallie kept her full attention to her meal, munching fries, wolfing down her huge cheeseburger.

Where did she put it all?

"You want to hit a movie after this?"

The girl shook her head.

Alex hated that his little girl's innocence had been tainted by a senseless act of violence.

"Gotta pee." Hallie jumped up and headed for the bathroom.

Inside, she closed herself into one of the two stalls. She waited impatiently for the woman in the next one to hurry up. A few moments later she heard water running as the lady washed her hands for what seemed an eternity.

Come on, come on! Hallie stood quietly, listening for the sound of the door. At last the dryer shut off, the door snicked open, then shut with a soft click.

Hallie closed her eyes and focused. She could do this. It was easy, once you learned how. She raised her fingers to her mouth and felt her stomach begin to heave in a familiar wave of motion. Then she leaned over the toilet, purging herself of everything she'd just eaten.

But not just the food.

Of everything bad that lay like a thick, black poison inside her.

Dear Reader,

Do you ever stop and think about how the course of our lives can change in an instant? I often think about that and wonder "What if?" What if a person made a different choice at one single moment along his or her life's journey? It fascinates me that one small action can drastically alter everything.

But sometimes the path we take is not by choice. Sometimes it's by accident, or a seemingly cruel twist of fate. Yet I've found that good can come from the proverbial dark cloud. When Caitlin Kramer suffers a severe accident, she's forced to take a long, hard look at her goals and dreams. At exactly what sort of person she is.

Alex Hunter has traveled a similar path. His main concern is protecting his daughter, and he'll go to any length to do it, including moving to the small Colorado mountain town of Deer Creek. Little does he know that fate has plans for him. And for Caitlin.

I hope you'll enjoy the twists and turns of Alex and Caitlin's journey to true love. Don't you just love a happy ending?

I enjoy hearing from my readers. You can e-mail me at BrendaMott@hotmail.com (please reference the book title on the subject line). Or stop by my author's page at the Smoky Mountain Romance Writers Web site at smrw.org or SuperAuthors.com. Happy reading!

Brenda Mott

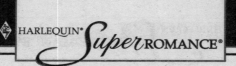

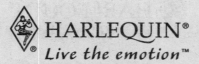

HARLEQUIN *Super*ROMANCE®

SUDDENLY A PARENT

FAMILY AT LAST
by K.N. Casper

Harlequin Superromance #1292

Adoption is a life-altering commitment.
Especially when you're single. And your new
son doesn't speak your language. But when
Jarrod hires Soviet-born linguist Nina Lockhart
to teach Sasha English, he has no idea
how complicated his life is about to become.

*Available in August 2005
wherever Harlequin books are sold.*

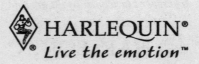

HARLEQUIN®
Live the emotion™